Acting Edition

The King Stag

Adapted from Carlo Gozzi's
Il Re Cervo

by Eberle Thomas &
Barbara Redmond

FOR PRODUCTION INQUIRIES

UNITED STATES AND CANADA
info@concordtheatricals.com
1-866-979-0447

UNITED KINGDOM AND EUROPE
licensing@concordtheatricals.co.uk
020-7054-7298

Each title is subject to availability from Concord Theatricals Corp.,
depending upon country of performance. Please be aware that *THE
KING STAG* may not be licensed by Concord Theatricals Corp. in
your territory. Professional and amateur producers should contact the
nearest Concord Theatricals Corp. office or licensing partner to verify
availability.

No one shall make any changes in this title(s) for the purpose of production. No part of this book may be reproduced, stored in a retrieval system, scanned, uploaded, or transmitted in any form, by any means, now known or yet to be invented, including mechanical, electronic, digital, photocopying, recording, videotaping, or otherwise, without the prior written permission of the publisher. No one shall share this title(s), or any part of this title(s), through any social media or file hosting websites.

For all inquiries regarding motion picture, television, online/digital and other media rights, please contact Concord Theatricals Corp.

MUSIC AND THIRD-PARTY MATERIALS USE NOTE

Licensees are solely responsible for obtaining formal written permission from copyright owners to use copyrighted music and/or other copyrighted third-party materials (e.g. artworks, logos) in the performance of this play and are strongly cautioned to do so. If no such permission is obtained by the licensee, then the licensee must use only original music and materials that the licensee owns and controls. Licensees are solely responsible and liable for clearances of all third-party copyrighted materials, including without limitation music, and shall indemnify the copyright owners of the play(s) and their licensing agent, Concord Theatricals Corp., against any costs, expenses, losses and liabilities arising from the use of such copyrighted third-party materials by licensees. For music, please contact the appropriate music licensing authority in your territory for the rights to any incidental music.

IMPORTANT BILLING AND CREDIT REQUIREMENTS

If you have obtained performance rights to this title, please refer to your licensing agreement for important billing and credit requirements.

Foreword

I had the good fortune to direct the premiere of this adaptation several years ago with a young cast that included several fine actors destined for distinguished careers in the theatre. The play is a winner. It captures the sheer fun of the Italian comic tradition; it offers something to delight both children and adults; and it allows for either elaborate or simple production values.

There is always a shortage of stageworthy material that is sufficiently respectful of young people to merit serious attention. Eberle Thomas and Barbara Redmond have done us all a favor by adding significantly to that repertoire.

May it find life on many, many stages!

Moses Goldberg
Producing Director, Stage One
Louisville, Kentucky
November, 1990

CHARACTERS

DERAMO, King of Serendippo
TARTAGLIA, Prime Minister
PANTALONE, The Exchequer
GENERAL SPAVENTO, Commander of the Army
LEANDRO, Chief of the Palace Guards
NORANDO THE GREAT, a Magician
TRUFFALDINO, His Assistant
ANGELA, Daughter of Pantalone
CLARICE, Sister of Tartaglia
SMERALDINA, Daughter of General Spavento
GUARDS
AN OLD HERMIT
A PARROT
THE KING STAG
A STATUE

Scenes and Settings

PROLOGUE
A street in Serendippo with three houses.

SCENE ONE
The palace gardens. An autumn morning.

SCENE TWO
The street. Shortly after.

SCENE THREE
The palace gardens. Later the same day.

SCENE FOUR
The street. The next morning.

SCENE FIVE
The Amber Forest. Afternoon of the same day.

SCENE SIX
The street. Evening of the same day.

SCENE SEVEN
The palace gardens. The same evening.

Scenes in the street are meant to be played "in one," in order to permit scene changes behind the curtain or other scenic device on which the street is depicted.

This play was commissioned by

THE ASOLO CHILDREN'S THEATRE.

THE KING STAG

PROLOGUE

(A street in Serendippo. Three houses, belonging to GENERAL SPAVENTO, TARTAGLIA and PANTALONE. Enter TRUFFALDINO with a map, lost)

TRUFFALDINO: Wow! Nyuh! Reading a book is hard enough, but reading a map! Nothing but squiggles and dots. *(Reading.)* "S-E-R-E . . . " *(Looking around at the street.)* I guess this must be the place. *(GENERAL SPAVENTO enters from his house.)* Aha! Maybe this gentleman can tell me. *(To GENERAL SPAVENTO.)* Excuse me. . .

GENERAL SPAVENTO: What?

TRUFFALDINO: I said, excuse me . . .

GENERAL SPAVENTO: Oh, no. Incorrect, improper, irregular. You should have said, "Excuse me, SIR!" On account of my rank, you know. Sorry, must be off now. Business, top secret, all that. Can't stop. Cheerio! *(GENERAL SPAVENTO exits.)*

TRUFFALDINO: *(Calling after General Spavento.)* But all I wanted to know is . . . *(Stops calling, realizing that the General has gone.)* . . . where am I? *(To audience.)* That wasn't very polite! What am I going to do now? *(TARTAGLIA enters from his house.)* Aha! *(To TARTAGLIA.)* Excuse me, SIR! I was wondering if you could tell me . . .

TARTAGLIA: *(With a characteristic stammer.)* Silence!

And stand absolutely still! (*TRUFFALDINO obeys.*) No one speaks to me in that familiar t-tone, b-boy. In fact, no one speaks to me at all, without my p-permission.

TRUFFALDINO: May I have your permission?

TARTAGLIA: No. Request denied. You are a foreigner, are you not?

TRUFFALDINO: I'm a stranger here, if that's what you mean.

TARTAGLIA: I don't like foreigners.

TRUFFALDINO: (*As HE raises one finger.*) But I only . . .

TARTAGLIA: Silence! And be still! (*TARTAGLIA exits, leaving TRUFFALDINO, mouth agape, with his forefinger pointing skyward. Enter PANTALONE from his house, humming a cheerful little tune.*)

PANTALONE: (*HE passes Truffaldino, "takes," stops singing abruptly and comes to a halt. To audience.*) That statue wasn't here last night. There's something not right about it, too. Funny looking, if you know what I mean. I shall have to look into it. (*PANTALONE starts to exit.*)

TRUFFALDINO: (*Still frozen, whispers.*) Sir. Please wait.

PANTALONE: (*Looking around and above.*) What?

TRUFFALDINO: Please, sir.

PANTALONE: (*Returning.*) Good heavens. It isn't a statue after all. What are you doing here, son?

TRUFFALDINO: (*Still frozen, whispering.*) May I speak to you, sir?

PANTALONE: Why, certainly.

TRUFFALDINO: (*Still frozen, but in full voice.*) Thank you. May I move around a little, too?

PANTALONE: What's the matter with you? Of course

you may move around.

TRUFFALDINO: (*Relaxing, shaking out the kinks.*) Oh, thank you. Very much. <u>Sir</u>! Now. What I wanted to ask you was, is this place Syra . . . Sarah . . . ?

PANTALONE: (*Trying to help.*) Syra . . . Sarah . . . Sahara? No. The Sahara, I believe, is a desert in the north of Africa. I'm afraid you're lost, son.

TRUFFALDINO: No. Not Sahara. Sarah . . . in . . . dumpo . . .

PANTALONE: Oh! Wait a minute. How do you spell it?

TRUFFALDINO: (*Reading from map.*) S-E-R-E-N . . .

PANTALONE: (*Reading over Truffaldino's shoulder.*) D-I-P . . .

TRUFFALDINO and PANTALONE: P-O!

PANTALONE: Right! This is it! (*Shakes TRUFFALDINO's hand.*) Welcome to the Kingdom of Serendippo. Have a pleasant stay. (*PANTALONE starts out.*)

TRUFFALDINO: Thank you.

PANTALONE: I must be going now. (*PANTALONE exits.*)

TRUFFALDINO: (*Calling after Pantalone.*) Goodbye! Thanks! (*To audience.*) Well! I feel better already! (*Remembering.*) Oh, dear! I should have asked him where the palace is. (*To audience.*) I'm supposed to meet my master there, and he doesn't like to be kept waiting! In fact . . .

VOICE OF NORANDO THE GREAT: (*Booming.*) TRUFFALDINO! TRUFFALDINO!

TRUFFALDINO: Hello. Oh. That's him. Where are you, sir?

VOICE OF NORANDO THE GREAT: Follow him. He's going to the palace.

TRUFFALDINO: Ah, the palace! Will you be there, too,

sir?

VOICE OF NORANDO THE GREAT: Follow him now, Truffaldino.

TRUFFALDINO: But, sir . . .

VOICE OF NORANDO THE GREAT: Silence! (*TRUFFALDINO shushes himself and audience.*) Follow him. To the palace.

TRUFFALDINO: (*Whispering.*) Follow him. (*To the audience.*) To the palace. (*HE exits, whispering.*) Follow him. To the palace. (*To the audience.*) Shhh! (*Exiting.*) Follow him. To the palace. (*Exits.*)

*

SCENE 1

(The palace gardens. At center a large fountain topped by the statue of a man. At right, a garden bench. At left, a wall of the palace with an entrance to the interior. As the scene opens, GENERAL SPAVENTO, TARTAGLIA and PANTALONE are all talking at once as KING DERAMO paces among them in confusion.)

KING DERAMO: *(Stops pacing.)*   Please, please, gentlemen! *(THEY subside.)* One at a time. Tartaglia?

TARTAGLIA: Well, I am, of c-course, unhappy that Your Majesty has taken such a d-drastic step without c-consulting me. Nevertheless, since you feel so strongly about it, I look favorably on this project.

KING DERAMO: Good. Thank you, Tartaglia. My lord Pantalone?

PANTALONE: I don't like it, Your Majesty. Sending for a magician! Why, it's entirely too risky. Most of them are frauds, for one thing. And even if this Norando the Great is the real thing, Serendippo is a lovely, peaceful kingdom. Why tamper with it by meddling about in magic?

KING DERAMO: *(Enthusiasm dampened.)* Well, it's not too late to send him away. What do YOU think, General?

GENERAL SPAVENTO: Well, I'm suspicious of magicians.

KING DERAMO: Yes, so am I, now.

GENERAL SPAVENTO: On the other hand, I'm a bit curious.

KING DERAMO: Well, yes. *(Shyly grinning.)* So am I.

GENERAL SPAVENTO: On the other hand, it could be dangerous.

KING DERAMO: Yes, it could be.

GENERAL SPAVENTO: On the other hand, consider our army with magical weapons. Invisible soldiers, invisible cannons. We could defeat any enemy without firing a shot. This magician might make Serendippo even more peaceful than it is now.

KING DERAMO: (*Enthusiastically.*) Yes, he might.

GENERAL SPAVENTO: On the other hand . . .

PANTALONE: Oh, stop it, General. How many hands have you got? Let's take a vote on it.

KING DERAMO: Good idea. Prime Minister?

TARTAGLIA: (*With thumb up.*) Yes. In favor. For your sake, Your Majesty. If you desire it, so do I.

KING DERAMO: Chancellor?

PANTALONE: (*With thumb down.*) Opposed.

KING DERAMO: Commander?

GENERAL SPAVENTO: (*Stretches thumb in various directions uncertainly.*) Well . . . (*Points thumb up.*) Yes. I say take the plunge.

KING DERAMO: Motion carried. Two to one. Marvelous.

LEANDRO: (*Entering.*) Your Majesty. The magician Norando and his servant have arrived.

KING DERAMO: Splendid! Show them in.

LEANDRO: (*Calling offstage.*) This way, please.

(*PANTALONE moves to join General Spavento near King Deramo. TARTAGLIA stands a bit aloof. NORANDO THE GREAT and TRUFFALDINO enter. A silence. TARTAGLIA moves to assume the position of intermediary.*)

TARTAGLIA: You are N-Norando, the famous magician?

NORANDO THE GREAT: I am. This is my loyal assistant and companion, Truffaldino.

TRUFFALDINO: (*Moving in a rapid circle to introduce himself.*) How do you do, gentlemen? That is, Your Excellencies, or Eminencies, or Majesties, as the case may be. Norando exaggerates when he calls me his assistant. I don't know a thing about magic. But if you'd like to play a game of cards, or roll some dice, or try a guessing game, I'm your man. In fact . . .

NORANDO THE GREAT: (*Gently.*) That's enough, Truffaldino.

TRUFFALDINO: He's right. I forgot to mention that I also talk too much, especially when . . .

NORANDO THE GREAT: Shhhhh.

TRUFFALDINO: Right. Shhhhh.

TARTAGLIA: (*Making introductions, impressively.*) Allow me to present Deramo, King of Serendippo. (*NORANDO THE GREAT and TRUFFALDINO bow.*) I am T-Tartaglia, his faithful Prime Minister. (*Slight pause.*) You may also bow to me. (*THEY do so.*) These other two gentlemen are Pantalone, our Royal Exchequer, and General Spavento, Commander of the Serendippo Army.

PANTALONE: Don't bother to bow to me. I'm just an old crock.

GENERAL SPAVENTO: Don't bow to me either. However, a salute would be nice. (*Exchange of salutes.*)

KING DERAMO: Now. If you will excuse me, my friends, I should like to speak to Norando in private.

PANTALONE: Of course, Your Majesty.

GENERAL SPAVENTO: If you should require my presence, sire, just say the word. (*To Norando.*) No offense, old chap. I'm sure your methods are completely on the up and up. But "Always be prepared." That's my motto.

PANTALONE: Come along, General. (*PANTALONE and GENERAL SPAVENTO exit.*)

TARTAGLIA: I think I should stay, Your Majesty.

KING DERAMO: That won't be necessary, Tartaglia. Thank you.

TARTAGLIA: Oh? (*Huffily.*) Very well. (*HE starts off.*)

NORANDO THE GREAT: Wait for me inside, Truffaldino.

TRUFFALDINO: Yes, sir. (*To Tartaglia, as THEY exit.*) Say, why don't we pop by the kitchen for a little snack? Nothing fancy: a glass of champagne, a nice leg of roasted chicken . . . (*A pause.*) How about peanut butter and jelly? (*THEY are gone.*)

KING DERAMO: (*Pacing a bit.*) Norando, I don't know whether you are justly famous for your magic or merely a fraud. But I'm going to take a chance on you. Because I need the help of . . . something beyond the usual powers of a man. In fact, I need the help of magic. (*Moves to fountain, resting a foot on it.*) You see this statue? My father. I would like to be as good a king as he was. My only wish is that Serendippo should remain the most peaceful kingdom ever known, and that my subjects should become the happiest on earth.

NORANDO THE GREAT: A good wish for a king to have.

KING DERAMO: But a king must be clever, a king must be shrewd! (*Laughs self-deprecatingly.*) I'm so gullible, Norando. If a traitor told me he was a patriot or a murderer claimed that he was a saint, I'd believe him!

NORANDO THE GREAT: You are young, Your Majesty.

KING DERAMO: Be that as it may, I must find some way of knowing whether people are what they seem to be. For instance: on his deathbed, my father made me swear that I would choose a bride who would be kind and honest and care more for the welfare of the kingdom than for herself. (*Sighs deeply.*) So far I have interviewed over five hundred young ladies. They all say they love me. They all say they love Serendippo. Are they all telling the truth? Even if they are, which one should I choose?

NORANDO THE GREAT: Sire. You ask for a magical solution to your problem. I can provide it.

KING DERAMO: Then you must!

NORANDO THE GREAT: But remember: magic alone is neither good nor evil. It must be used wisely or it becomes dangerous. More dangerous than you can imagine.

KING DERAMO: I promise you that I shall use it wisely and well.

NORANDO THE GREAT: Then I shall reveal two magical secrets to you. (*Moving to the statue.*) First, this statue of your father has the power of acting as a Test of Truth. (*Touches statue and mumbles.*) Kalzuth, Zerath. (*To Deramo.*) When you wish to know whether someone speaks honestly, pass your hand over the statue's eyes. (*HE does so. The eyes of the STATUE open.*) The statue will respond to any lie spoken in its presence.

KING DERAMO: What do you mean?

NORANDO THE GREAT: Watch closely. "My name is King Deramo." (*The STATUE smiles and shakes his head.*)

KING DERAMO: Amazing! You've saved my life, Norando.

NORANDO THE GREAT: To return the statue to its normal state, just close its eyes. (*HE does so.*)

KING DERAMO: Excellent! And the other secret?

NORANDO THE GREAT: (*Produces a black and gold card*.) The other is more powerful and far more dangerous. You see here a verse of incantation. With this verse, you may transport yourself into the body of another creature. Disguised as a cat, a bird, a beggar, you may travel freely among your subjects unrecognized. And you should thus be able to distinguish, as you put it, traitors from patriots and murderers from saints.

KING DERAMO: (*Taking card*.) I thank you with all my heart. Serendippo will now become all that I long for it to be.

NORANDO THE GREAT: We shall see.

KING DERAMO: (*Moving toward the palace*.) Leandro! Tell my ministers to return at once!

LEANDRO: (*Offstage*.) Yes, Your Majesty!

NORANDO THE GREAT: Your Majesty, I must warn you: do not reveal the secret of transformation to another living soul.

KING DERAMO: But why?

NORANDO THE GREAT: Sire! You have aptly diagnosed your own weakness: you are gullible. Keep the secret SECRET.

KING DERAMO: I shall. I promise. (*Enter TARTAGLIA, PANTALONE and GENERAL SPAVENTO, speaking at once*.)

TARTAGLIA: What is it, sire?

PANTALONE: You called, Your Majesty?

GENERAL SPAVENTO: No trouble, I hope.

KING DERAMO: My friends, this is a glorious day for Serendippo. I am now able to promise you that I shall choose my queen within the week. (*All respond enthusiastically*.) In fact, I shall begin by considering ladies of your own families—your sister, Tartaglia, and the daughters of Pantalone and the General. Tell them that I shall see them here in the garden this afternoon.

TARTAGLIA: Very good, Your Majesty. I am sure my sister, C-Clarice, will d-delight you.

GENERAL SPAVENTO: Well, my daughter Smeraldina's quite a catch.

NORANDO THE GREAT: Good luck, Your Majesty.

KING DERAMO: But Norando! You're not leaving!

NORANDO THE GREAT: Oh, I'll be seeing you again, I expect. For the time being, you're on your own, sire. Good day, gentlemen. (*HE bows and exits.*)

KING DERAMO: Go, my lords. Let your daughters and sisters know what I have decided. I swear I'll show no favorites. The first truthful, loving woman I meet shall be my queen.

TARTAGLIA: My sister will be here within the hour, sire. (*TARTAGLIA exits.*)

GENERAL SPAVENTO: Smeraldina's a charmer. Don't make up your mind before you see her, Your Majesty. (*GENERAL SPAVENTO exits.*)

PANTALONE: Thank you, sire. I'll tell Angela that you're expecting her. (*PANTALONE exits.*)

KING DERAMO: (*Alone, laughs joyfully.*) King Deramo is free of doubts at last! What will they say of me? "Deramo the Just"? "Deramo the Wise"? "Deramo the Good"? (*To the statue, as HE opens its eyes.*) What do you say, Father? "My name is Norando the Great." (*The STATUE smiles and shakes his head. KING DERAMO laughs.*) You're right, Father. Just as you always were. (*HE laughs.*)

*

 THE KING STAG

SCENE 2

(A street in Serendippo, as in Prologue, revealing three houses belonging to General Spavento, Tartaglia and Pantalone. Enter GENERAL SPAVENTO and PANTALONE, heading home to tell their daughters of their forthcoming interviews with the King.)

GENERAL SPAVENTO: I can't wait to tell Smeraldina! You know, deep down in my heart I've always believed that my daughter would become the Queen. And you may recall, my lord Pantalone, that royalty runs in my family.

PANTALONE: Everyone runs in your family, General. Especially on the battlefield.

GENERAL SPAVENTO: What's that?

PANTALONE: Joke.

GENERAL SPAVENTO: Are you accusing the noble line of Spavento of cowardice?

PANTALONE: Oh, no. I was applauding your instinct for self-preservation.

GENERAL SPAVENTO: I see. Well, that's a horse of a different color.

PANTALONE: You said it. And the color's yellow.

GENERAL SPAVENTOL: Yellow? Is that an insult or . . . joke?

PANTALONE: Joke. So long, General. See you at the palace. *(PANTALONE exits into his house.)*

GENERAL SPAVENTO: Right-o. May the best man win. Or the best girl. Or the best man's best girl. *(To audience.)* Whatever's fair. I believe in fair play. I always say: It's not how you lose, it's what game you play that counts. *(That didn't sound quite right.)* At least, I think that's what I always say. (*GENERAL SPAVENTO starts to enter his house as TARTAGLIA appears.*)

TARTAGLIA: Wait. G-general. A word with you.

GENERAL SPAVENTO: (*Suspiciously.*) Yes?

TARTAGLIA: I must remind you. According to protocol, the Prime Minister outranks all other state officials. C-correct?

GENERAL SPAVENTO: Correct.

TARTAGLIA: In that case, my sister, C-clarice, should be allowed the first interview with the K-king. C-correct?

GENERAL SPAVENTO: C- . . . Right.

TARTAGLIA: Don't worry, G-general. When my sister becomes Q-queen, I'll use my influence to upgrade the army. (*Secretly.*) With the right sort of army, Serendippo c-could c-conquer the entire c-continent! Think of it! A war to end all wars! You think about it.

GENERAL SPAVENTO: Right.

TARTAGLIA: C-carry on, G-general. (*HE salutes and exits to his house.*)

GENERAL SPAVENTO: (*Alone.*) War? (*Shudders.*) Frightening fellow, that.

(*GENERAL SPAVENTO exits to his house. Enter NORANDO THE GREAT with TRUFFALDINO. NORANDO pauses and observes the three houses curiously, as if able to see inside.*)

TRUFFALDINO: (*Not noticing Norando's preoccupation, pushing a large trunk across the stage.*) Ahhh! Breathe that delicious fresh air, sir. You know, this little town has a charm all its own. And we could do with a bit of a rest, don't you think, sir? Why don't we just settle in here for a couple of days—eat, drink, sleep, relax, go fishing, tell a few jokes, crack a few nuts . . .

NORANDO THE GREAT: (*Silencing him.*) Truffaldino.

TRUFFADINO: Sir?

NORANDO THE GREAT: I agree.

TRUFFALDINO: Good. Agree with what?

NORANDO THE GREAT: We should remain here awhile. Something interesting is about to happen. I'd like to see how it all turns out.

TRUFFALDINO: Well, as coincidence would have it, sir, I passed a nice, clean cozy inn this morning. "Hot Meals and Soft Beds," the sign said. Doesn't that sound inviting?

NORANDO THE GREAT: Yes. But if I am to observe this little drama more closely, you must go to the inn alone.

TRUFFALDINO: Couldn't I stay with you, sir? I don't much like being by myself.

NORANDO THE GREAT: Don't be afraid. Now listen carefully. I shall leave instructions for you during my absence. You must follow them exactly.

TRUFFALDINO: Where will I find these instructions?

NORANDO THE GREAT: Wherever you are. Be sure that you obey them quickly and precisely. You understand?

TRUFFALDINO: Yes, sir. But before you . . . (*HE turns away from Norando to point in the direction of the inn.*) . . . why not come along to the inn with me—it's just down the way— and get a bite to eat, to tide you over?

NORANDO THE GREAT: Without hesitation, without preparation! (*LIGHTNING flash. NORANDO THE GREAT disappears. Near where he stood is a parrot with a note in his beak.*)

TRUFFALDINO: (*Looking up at the sky.*) Holy cow! That was some storm. Now, what I was saying, sir, was . . (*Turns, "takes".*) Sir? Sir? He's gone. (*To audience.*)

That's the trouble with working for a magician. He gets bored with your conversation, he pulls the old disappearing act. (*Sees parrot.*) Hello. What's this? A parrot! (*Calls.*) Anybody lose a parrot? (*Sees note.*) What's that you've got in your mouth, Polly? Why, it's a piece of paper. Don't eat paper, Polly. It'll give you indigestion. (*Removes paper and starts to throw it away. "Takes".*) Wait a minute! It's a note. (*Reads.*) "Message from Norando to Truffaldino." (*Opens note, reads.*) "Take this parrot with you to the inn. Buy him a bowl of water and a plate of crackers." Well, I'll be a monkey's uncle. (*Taking the parrot onto his hand.*) Okay, my little friend. All aboard. (*Starts to exit toward the inn.*) Well, what do you have to say for yourself?

PARROT: Hel-lo. Hel-lo.

TRUFFALDINO: He talks! Say, did you hear the one about the elephant who forgot to pack his trunk . . ? (*TRUFFALDINO laughs wildly at his own joke as THEY approach the exit. Enter SMERALDINA, dressed up, with GENERAL SPAVENTO. TRUFFALDINO halts.*)

SMERALDINA: Really? Really and truly? You don't think it's too gaudy?

GENERAL SPAVENTO: No, no, child. The dress is fine.

SMERALDINA: And the earrings?

GENERAL SPAVENTO: Just right. Come along now.

TRUFFALDINO: (*Who has stopped, smitten with Smeraldina.*) Excuse me, sir. I must speak to this lady.

GENERAL SPAVENTO: Yes?

SMERALDINA: Well?

TRUFFALDINO: You may not believe this, but my master—the magician Norando—once told me that I was destined to marry a beautiful girl with red hair.

GENERAL SPAVENTO: (*After a brief pause.*) And . . ?

TRUFFALDINO: And I am delighted to announce, miss, that I have fallen madly in love with you.

SMERALDINA: (*Pleased in spite of herself, laughs.*) Is that so? You know something?

TRUFFALDINO: What?

SMERALDINA: You're peculiar.

GENERAL SPAVENTO: Look here, old chap. No offence, but this is . . . well, you know . . . highly irregular, so to speak. And we're in a bit of a rush at the moment.

SMERALDINA: Yes. You see, I'm going to be the Queen.

TRUFFALDINO: Queen? You mean, you're going to marry . . . ?

SMERALDINA: King Deramo. That's right. (*TRUFFALDINO sobs.*)

GENERAL SPAVENTO: Sorry, lad. Chin up. Stiff upper. All that.

SMERALDINA: Cheer up. You're peculiar, but you're cute. (*As SHE exits with GENERAL SPAVENTO, grandly.*) I shall always remember you with fondness. (*THEY are gone. TRUFFALDINO makes one last enormous sob, then recovers completely.*)

TRUFFALDINO: Let's go, Polly. By the way, did you hear the joke about the rope?

THE PARROT: No.

TRUFFALDINO: Then let's skip it. (*THEY exit, TRUFFALDINO laughing wildly. Enter LEANDRO stealthily. HE tosses a pebble at the window of Tartaglia's house.*)

LEANDRO: Clarice! Clarice!

CLARICE: (*Appearing at the window.*) What is it? Oh! Leandro! (*SHE weeps.*) Please go away. If my brother finds you here . . . Oh, it's awful! You don't know what's happened.

LEANDRO: Yes, I do. But listen to me, Clarice. I know King Deramo. Just tell him the truth. Tell him that you love me. Everything will be all right, I swear to you.

CLARICE: But my brother made me promise that . . .

TARTAGLIA: (*Entering through his front door.*) So! You again! What are you doing here?

LEANDRO: Leaving.

TARTAGLIA: Wait! (*To Clarice.*) Clarice, c-come down immediately. Hurry! (*SHE disappears from window.*) Now let's get this clear, young man. You have no business here. Clarice is not for you. She is the sister of the Prime Minister, soon to be your Q-queen, whereas you are a mere palace guard.

LEANDRO: I love Clarice and she loves me!

TARTAGLIA: Watch your t-tongue! (*To Clarice, as SHE enters from the front door.*) C-clarice, I absolutely forbid you to see this fellow again. Do you understand?

CLARICE: (*Sadly.*) Yes.

TARTAGLIA: (*To Leandro.*) Goodbye.

LEANDRO: But . . .

TARTAGLIA: Goodb-b-bye! (*LEANDRO, enraged, exits.*) Now, to the palace. Hurry up, Clarice, and take that sick look off your face.

PANTALONE: (*Entering with ANGELA.*) Come along, Angela.

TARTAGLIA: Ah. Angela! (*Leaving Clarice and approaching Angela.*) Good day, Miss Angela. Lord Pantalone. A beautiful day. (*To Angela.*) Although there is no beauty that can compete with yours, if I may say so, Miss Angela. Pantalone, I presume you know that the rules of protocol dictate that my sister should receive the first interview with the King?

PANTALONE: Very well.

TARTAGLIA: Once the King has chosen C-clarice for his Q-queen—which is a forgone conclusion, I'm sure you'll agree—I hope that you will do me the honor of consenting to my request for your daughter's hand in marriage. We could perhaps arrange a double wedding?

PANTALONE: I'll think it over.

TARTAGLIA: And what about you, my darling Angela? Would it make you happy to marry me?

ANGELA: It will make me happy to marry a man of whom my father approves.

TARTAGLIA: Well spoken. Until later, then, my dear. We must be off. C-come, C-clarice. (*Whispering fiercely as they move off.*) Take that hangdog look off your face. Smile, for heaven's sake! (*TARTAGLIA and CLARICE exit.*)

ANGELA: Father, I want you to know. I would never marry that man.

PANTALONE: My dear, I'd disinherit you if you did. Let's go now. We mustn't keep His Majesty waiting. (*PANTALONE notices that ANGELA lags behind.*) What's is it?

ANGELA: It's so embarrassing, Father. I dread it!

PANTALONE: But why?

ANGELA: Oh, you don't understand.

PANTALONE: Understand what, child?

ANGELA: (*Simply.*) I love Deramo. I always have.

PANTALONE: Oh. I see . . .

ANGELA: Think of all the beautiful young ladies in the kingdom, all of them vying to be Queen. He'll never choose me. It will be so humiliating.

PANTALONE: My poor girl. You take a dim view of your chances, I must say.

ANGELA: But, Father . . .

PANTALONE: Well, you're probably wise. Don't get your hopes up. Come along now. (*THEY start out.*) Everybody has a share of sadness in this life, you know, Angela. You'll get over it. Come along and be a brave girl. That's it. (*THEY are gone. Enter TRUFFALDINO, with PARROT.*)

TRUFFALDINO: I wish we'd hear something from Norando, Polly. This habit he has of appearing and disappearing without so much as a howdy-doo, I just never know what to expect, especially when . . . (*A note pops out of one of the walls.*)

PARROT: Look-out. Look-out.

TRUFFALDINO: What? What?

PARROT: Mes-sage! Mes-sage!

TRUFFALDINO: Message? Mes . . . Why do you say everything twice? (*Sees message, "takes".*) Oh, for goodness sake! (*Gets note and reads.*) "Norando to Truffaldino: Take parrot to palace gardens." Take parrot to palace gardens? Oh! A royal summons, Pol. You're headed for the big time! Oh, this is exciting. Come on, let's make tracks! (*They exit.*)

*

SCENE 3

*(The palace gardens, as in Scene One. A small table
has been placed near the bench, right, with a pitcher of
water and goblets on it. KING DERAMO enters,
perusing a piece of paper. HE glances at the statue
and moves to it.)*

KING DERAMO: Now I shall know the truth. *(Paces,
musing.)* Is that always good, I wonder? Suppose I were to
fall hopelessly in love with one of these ladies? And suppose
she did not return my love? Would I not then prefer to hear a
lie—a gentle lie—rather than the harsh truth? *(Moving briskly
back to the statue.)* No! The truth is better! It is my duty to
insist upon the truth! *(KING DERAMO returns to his reading,
as LEANDRO enters, carrying the parrot.)*
LEANDRO: Your Majesty, the ladies have arrived.
KING DERAMO: Good.
LEANDRO: I have been advised by the Prime Minister
that, according to protocol, Miss Clarice is entitled to the first
audience.
KING DERAMO: Ah, yes, protocol. Well, why not?
Send her in.
LEANDRO: And the magician's man, Truffaldino, has
brought this parrot.
KING DERAMO: A parrot?
LEANDRO: He says that it is a gift from Norando the
Great and that it must be kept here in the gardens.
KING DERAMO: Indeed? Well, I suppose we'd best
leave it here, then, Leandro. *(KING DERAMO points out a
niche on the wall near the palace entrance.)* Tell Clarice that
I am ready to receive her.

LEANDRO: Yes, sire. (*LEANDRO puts parrot down and exits.*)

KING DERAMO: (*Studying parrot.*) Norando has not forgotten me, at least. (*Seeing CLARICE standing in doorway.*) Ah, Clarice! Come in, please, won't you?

CLARICE: (*Entering nervously.*) Yes, sire.

KING DERAMO: Don't be afraid.

CLARICE: (*Startled.*) What?

KING DERAMO: (*A bit nervous himself.*) I said, don't be afraid.

CLARICE: Oh. No. I'm not . . . afraid.

KING DERAMO: Good. Sit down. (*Motions her to fountain as HE moves to small table at right.*) This is . . . rather awkward.

CLARICE: (*Still standing uneasily at center.*) What?

KING DERAMO: This is rather awkward, don't you think? (*Pours himself a glass of water.*) Such an unnatural way to choose a wife.

CLARICE: Unnatural?

KING DERAMO: Yes. You see, I must interview you as if I . . . as if I were hiring you as a chambermaid or a cook. It's not very romantic, is it? (*Pouring a second glass of water.*) Sit, please, sit.

CLARICE: Oh, yes. (*SHE sits.*) But if you don't like doing it this way, sire, why do you do it?

KING DERAMO: Because . . . Well, let's not go into that just now. Would you like a drink of water?

CLARICE: No thank you, sire.

KING DERAMO: But I've already poured. Two cups. Wouldn't you like one?

CLARICE: Oh. Yes. Very much. (*SHE takes water, gulps it down.*) Thank you, Your Majesty.

KING DERAMO: (*Returning to table to put glass down.*)
Well. Where shall I begin? I must choose a wife.

CLARICE: (*Rapidly, tensely.*) Yes, sire.

KING DERAMO: And who could be a worthier choice
than the daughter of my beloved Prime Minister?

CLARICE: Yes, sire. I mean, no, sire. I mean . . . me?

KING DERAMO: Yes, Clarice, you. But first I must ask
you three questions. (*Picks up sheet of paper.*) And please
answer truthfully. My Queen, you see, must be honest—not
just with me, but with everyone.

CLARICE: Yes, sire.

KING DERAMO: (*Moves to statue, opens its eyes.*) Here
is the first question. (*Reads.*) "Would it please you to become
Queen of Serendippo?"

CLARICE: Please me . . . to be Queen? . . . Yes. I think
it would.

KING DERAMO: (*Looks at statue. No response.*) Good.
The second question, then. (*Reads.*) "Which is more
important: a good life for all citizens of Serendippo, or your
own personal happiness?"

CLARICE: (*Relaxing, answering openly.*) I think it's
more important for ALL the people to have a good life. Of
course, I'd like to be happy, too, but I don't suppose that's
nearly so important.

KING DERAMO: (*Consults statue, which does not
respond.*) That's a good answer, Clarice. Now the final
question—and this is of great concern to me. (*Reads.*) "Could
you trust, respect and love me as a husband?"

CLARICE: (*Panics.*) What? Trust you, Your Majesty?
Oh, certainly, everyone trusts you . . .

KING DERAMO: The question is, "Could you trust,
respect and . . ."

CLARICE: Respect? Oh, yes, sire. I respect you very much . . .

KING DERAMO: And love? (*A pause.*) Do you love me, Clarice?

CLARICE: I . . . I . . . Oh! My throat's so dry I can scarcely speak!

KING DERAMO: (*Moving to table.*) Have a little more water. (*HE pours.*)

CLARICE: (*Aside.*) What shall I do? My brother said that I must convince him that I love him! It's terrible.

KING DERAMO: (*Returning to CLARICE with goblet.*) Here, Clarice. Drink this.

CLARICE: Thank you, sire. (*SHE drains it at a gulp again.*)

KING DERAMO: Now, Clarice. Do you love me?

CLARICE: (*Pause.*) Yes, Your Majesty.

KING DERAMO: (*Looks at STATUE, which smiles and shakes its head.*) I see. My dear Clarice, perhaps you say that because you do not wish to embarrass or offend your King. Tell me, are you not in love with someone else?

CLARICE: (*Aside.*) My brother is so cruel! He forces me to lie. (*To Deramo, ashamedly.*) No, Your Majesty. I love only you.

KING DERAMO: (*Looks at STATUE, which responds again.*) Well, Clarice. (*HE closes the statue's eyes.*) I have listened carefully, and I believe I know what is truly in your heart. But now I must see the other ladies who are waiting. Thank you. You may go.

CLARICE: (*Turns on her way to the door.*) Your Majesty, may I ask YOU something?

KING DERAMO: Of course.

CLARICE: What chance is there that you will choose me

as your bride?

KING DERAMO: Honestly? (*Gently.*) It is not likely.

CLARICE: (*Happily.*) Oh, thank you, sire! (*SHE runs out.*)

KING DERAMO: (*Slow "take".*) I must say she took the bad news well. (*Calls.*) Leandro! Send in the next lady.

LEANDRO: (*Offstage.*) Yes, sire.

KING DERAMO: (*To statue.*) You do very well at this game of truth, Father.

SMERALDINA: (*Entering with a flourish.*) Your Majesty—exalted, reverenced and magniloquent Majesty—I am your most devoted servant. (*Curtseys very low.*)

KING DERAMO: Ah, Smeraldina. Come in, my dear.

SMERALDINA: Why, you called me "dear." Well, you're very sweet too, Your Majesty. I knew we'd hit it off right away. I'll be a marvelous wife for you, sire, and a magnificent queen. My father says that . . .

KING DERAMO: Excuse me, Smeraldina. Before we continue our conversation, won't you please sit down?

SMERALDINA: Certainly, my dear. (*Moves toward bench at right.*) Now that we've gotten so well acquainted, why don't we BOTH sit down . . .

KING DERAMO: No, Smeraldina, not there!

SMERALDINA: What?

KING DERAMO: Over here. (*Indicating fountain.*) Would you please sit over here?

SMERALDINA: (*Smiles.*) My, my! You ARE going to be a bossy sort of husband, aren't you? All right, I'll sit over here. (*SHE does so.*) You're very attractive, did you know that?

KING DERAMO: Uh . . . Smeraldina. I must ask you a question or two. . .

SMERALDINA: Anything, anything at all.

KING DERAMO: (*Opening statue's eyes.*) But please consider your answers carefully . . .

SMERALDINA: (*As SHE interrupts, the STATUE begins to smile and shake its head vigorously.*) Oh, yes, of course, Your Majesty. I never say ANYTHING without giving it a great deal of thought. That's a characteristic of all the Spaventos, as you may have already noticed . . .

KING DERAMO: (*A bit rattled by her non-stop talk accompanied by the STATUE's vigorous response.*) Wait, wait, Smeraldina! Let me caution you: speak with absolute honesty, without the least . . .

SMERALDINA: Oh, I'm always honest, why, I've never told a single fib in all my life . . . (*THE STATUE responds as before.*)

KING DERAMO: Smeraldina! Please. I'll ask you just one question. And try to answer it as frankly as you can. (*Reads from paper.*) "Do you have a truly DEEP affection for me as a . . ."

SMERALDINA: (*SHE continues without pause, with STATUE accompaniment.*) Oh, good heavens, yes! And DEEP? The Spaventos are notorious for the depth of their passions. Deep as the ocean, that's us. And I think I might add, without being accused of vanity because really everyone knows it to be the truth, that we're an unusually handsome family, as you, in your great discernment, may have noticed, sire. Blood will tell, don't you think, especially Blood Royal, as they say. Because, you know, my great-great-great-grandfather, after all, was a king, himself. In Castille, I think, or was it Persia? Well, anyway, before him, all the Spaventos were kings and queens, every single one. Why, when you and I are married, it will be as if I were simply COMING HOME after all these years. Some people have that certain something, don't you agree? I'm one of them. I'm what you might call "throne prone." It's going to be beautiful, Your Majesty, so very . . .

KING DERAMO: *(Dizzied by her monologue and the STATUE's activity.)* Please, Smeraldina, just be quiet for a moment and listen to . . .

SMERALDINA: *(As before.)* Oh, I've always been a quiet girl. If there's one thing I can't stand it's someone who's always talking. Why, sometimes I go off to my room alone and spend hours and hours not uttering a single sound. Just thinking. It's what you might call a love of contemplation. Everyone in our family has it, but it's more highly developed in my case, I think, because . . .

KING DERAMO: *(Reeling, shouts.)* Silence! *(SHE is silenced.)* And . . . *(Under his breath, to the statue, as he "turns it off".)* . . . you, too. Well, Smeraldina. You're a charming girl. And I shall certainly keep you in mind when I make a decision. You may go now.

SMERALDINA: You mean, that's all?

KING DERAMO: Yes. Thank you.

SMERALDINA: Oh, no. Thank YOU, Your Majesty. Did I tell you—you're very attractive, sire. And I'm a very lucky girl.

KING DERAMO: That's true. Why don't you go and find some place to be alone so you can contemplate?

SMERALDINA: Oh, yes, that's a lovely idea. I'll contemplate my wedding gown. Farewell, Your Majesty . . . for now.

KING DERAMO: Goodbye, Smeraldina.

SMERALDINA: In future, we shall look back upon this moment with great tenderness . . .

KING DERAMO: Goodbye, Smeraldina.

SMERALDINA: Posterity will commemorate this day in verse and song . . .

KING DERAMO: Goodbye . . .

SMERALDINA: . . . in great romantic dramas . . .

KING DERAMO: Good . . .

SMERALDINA: Our children and our children's children . . .

KING DERAMO: Smeraldina!

SMERALDINA: Hmm?

KING DERAMO: Shh! Time to contemplate. In silence. And solitude.

SMERALDINA: True, sire. I go. Farewell. (*SHE exits.*)

KING DERAMO: Whew! (*To the statue.*) Father, I begin to despair. Shall I ever find a woman who's sincere?

LEANDRO: (*Entering.*) Would you like to see the last young lady, Your Majesty?

KING DERAMO: Oh. Yes, Leandro. (*Absently.*) Who is it?

LEANDRO: The Lady Angela, sire. Daughter of Lord Pantalone.

KING DERAMO: (*Brightening.*) Ah. Ask her to enter.

LEANDRO: Yes, sire. (*HE exits.*)

KING DERAMO: Angela. Such a lovely girl. We've seldom spoken, but there's something about her . . . (*To statue.*) Forgive me, Father, but I hope I shan't see that smile of yours again. I hope that Angela . . . (*Enter ANGELA. KING DERAMO stops short, sensing her presence. A slight pause.*) Angela. Please sit down.

ANGELA: Thank you, sire. (*ANGELA sits at the fountain.*)

KING DERAMO: (*Taking a sip of water to steel himself.*)

It is my duty, Angela, to ask you some questions. Forgive me.

ANGELA: Forgive?

KING DERAMO: For being . . . so formal.

ANGELA: That's only proper. You are the King, I am your subject.

KING DERAMO: Ah, yes. Well. First question: would you be pleased if I were to choose you as my Queen?

ANGELA: (*Calmly, not looking at him.*) Yes, sire.

KING DERAMO: Good. Oh, stupid!

ANGELA: I beg your pardon?

KING DERAMO: I, uh, overlooked something. (*Opening STATUE's eyes.*) Could you say that again?

ANGELA: Say what, sire?

KING DERAMO: That it would please you to . . . you know.

ANGELA: To be your Queen?

KING DERAMO: Yes. (*Smiles weakly.*) Would you say it again?

ANGELA: (*A bit embarrassed.*) It would please me to be your Queen.

KING DERAMO: (*Looks at statue. No response.*) Good! Very good! The second question. Which is more important: the welfare of all the people or your own happiness.

ANGELA: The welfare of everyone.

KING DERAMO: (*Looks at statue. No response. Pats statue affectionately.*) Excellent. Well, now we come to the third and final question. Could you . . . Is it possible . . . That is . . . (*Pause. HE suddenly kneels before her.*) Do you love me?

ANGELA: (*Looking into his eyes.*) Yes. Yes!

KING DERAMO: You do? Then . . . (*About to embrace her, HE stops suddenly.*) Oh, blast it! I forgot! One moment, please. (*Rises, looks at statue.*) I'm sorry. I must ask you once more. Do you love me?

ANGELA: This is cruel, sire.

KING DERAMO: No, please! Don't be offended. You needn't answer. I'll . . .

ANGELA: No, you have asked, and I shall answer. (*Pause. KING DERAMO looks at the statue fearfully.*) I do. Love you.

KING DERAMO: (*Seeing no response from the statue, turns a bit giddy. HE begins to smile broadly and sinks to his knees beside Angela.*) Ah, yes, you do! That's . . . wonderful!

ANGELA: But, sire, why are you smiling . . . so strangely?

KING DERAMO: Because . . .(*Pointing at statue, almost shouts.*) . . . HE isn't smiling! (*Laughs, kisses Angela's hand. Rises and bounds to the palace entrance.*) Leandro! Leandro!

LEANDRO: (*Entering at a run.*) Yes, sire?

KING DERAMO: Quickly! Call them all in! All my ministers!

LEANDRO: At once, Your Majesty.

KING DERAMO: Be quick! Hurry! (*As LEANDRO exits, KING DERAMO rushes back to Angela.*) Come, Angela. (*Helps her up.*) We must greet them.

ANGELA: But, sire, I don't understand.

KING DERAMO: Oh, forgive me! In my excitement, I forgot to say . . . I love YOU, Angela.

ANGELA: You do?

KING DERAMO: I do, and I shall, as long as flowers bloom and stars still shine.

ANGELA: (*Almost faints, sinks back down against fountain.*) Oh! Your Majesty! (*KING DERAMO and*

*ANGELA burst into joyful, helpless laughter. Enter, led by
LEANDRO, TARTAGLIA, CLARICE, PANTALONE,
GENERAL SPAVENTO and SMERALDINA. The ministers
talk at once.)*

TARTAGLIA: What is it, Your Majesty?

PANTALONE: May we assist you, sire?

GENERAL SPAVENTO: Any little thing we should
know, sire?

KING DERAMO: (*Taking Angela by the hand as THEY
try to compose themselves.*) My lords, I have chosen! Angela
shall be my bride.

TARTAGLIA: Angela! Is this a plot against me, sire?

KING DERAMO: No, Tartaglia . . .

TARTAGLIA: (*Pointing at Pantalone.*) This rotten old
man has always envied me. He wants to be P-prime Minister!
He's made his d-daughter trick you!

KING DERAMO: Not at all, Tartaglia.   Norando the
Great has . . .

TARTAGLIA: Norando the Great! A magician! A fraud!
Useless! Foolish!

KING DERAMO: No, listen to me, Tartaglia, and I will
convince you that Norando is no fraud. He has placed in my
hands two priceless secrets. One of them is a magical means
of determining the truth. This statue has been charmed so that
it will smile when anyone speaks falsely in its presence.
Watch! (*Opens STATUE's eyes.*) "I hate Angela with all my
heart." (*STATUE smiles and shakes head.*) You see? (*Closes
STATUE's eyes.*) By this method I learned the truth within the
hearts of Clarice and Smeraldina. Both are lovely ladies, but
neither of them truly loves me. Angela DOES, and Angela
shall be my Queen.

TARTAGLIA: You mean that c-crumbling p-pile of rocks

laughed at my sister?

KING DERAMO: Of course not, Tartaglia. Please, everyone, take joy in our marriage. Tomorrow we shall celebrate with a Royal Hunt in the Amber Forest. Will you accompany us, General Spavento?

GENERAL SPAVENTO: Of course! I'm not offended by your choice, sire. After all, fair play's the thing! And Smeraldina is still quite a catch, if I do say so myself. Some lucky fellow will grab her yet.

KING DERAMO: Good. Lord Pantalone, you'll join the hunt, I trust? Perhaps you can teach me a thing or two about shooting.

PANTALONE: As I'm to be your father-in-law, sire, I suppose I ought to keep my eye on you.

GENERAL SPAVENTO: (*To Pantalone.*) Oh, you can leave the teaching to me, old boy. (*To all.*) I'm the crack shot around here, after all. Did I ever tell you about the time I hit an elephant in India . . . ?

PANTALONE: You did, General. Yes. Several times.

KING DERAMO: And you, my dear Tartaglia? (*Making up to him.*) My faithful Prime Minister and my friend? Please say you'll come.

TARTAGLIA: I wouldn't miss it, Your Majesty.

KING DERAMO: Splendid! And you, too, Leandro.

LEANDRO: Thank you, sire. And if you will permit me, I should like to take this opportunity of making a request of the Prime Minister. (*KING DERAMO nods.*) My Lord Tartaglia, although I am not of noble birth, I love your sister Clarice and wish to wed her. Will you honor me by . . . ?

TARTAGLIA: No. Never! Insults! Nothing but insults!

KING DERAMO: Please, please! No disagreements today. (*To Leandro.*) When the Prime Minister's temper has cooled, Leandro, perhaps he will reconsider your proposal. Now, my lords, ladies, let us go in to dine. A feast to celebrate the happiest day of Deramo's life!

ANGELA: And of mine.

GENERAL SPAVENTO: Good show! Three cheers: hip-hip . . .

ALL: Hurrah! (*ALL except TARTAGLIA exit in high spirits, speaking the following lines simultaneously.*)

CLARICE: (*To Angela.*) Oh, Angela! I'm so happy for you.

SMERALDINA: It's wonderful, Angela.

CLARICE: Have you set a date?

SMERALDINA: Have you thought about a wedding gown?

GENERAL SPAVENTO: Your daughter's a lucky girl, old man.

PANTALONE: I think the King's luck is pretty good, too, if I may say so.

GENERAL SPAVENTO: Smeraldina didn't really put her heart into it, you know.

PANTALONE: Really?

GENERAL SPAVENTO: Yes, she's like me: modest, shy, reserved . . . (*THEY exit, leaving TARTAGLIA alone.*)

TARTAGLIA: D-deramo has done it now! Insulted my sister! Snatched my beloved Angela from me! I'll be revenged! Tomorrow, in the Amber Forest, there's going to be a hunting accident. D-deramo must d-die! Agh! I'm in such a rage, I could kill them all! Even . . . (*Eying the parrot.*) . . . this p-putrid little p-parrot! What do you say, tweetie-bird? I've a good mind to . . . (*Draws dagger.*) . . . chop you up and feed you to my c-cat. What'ya think of that?

PARROT: Not much.

TARTAGLIA: Oh, a wiseacre, eh? Well, you c-can c-consider yourself lucky that I'm not stupid enough to w-waste my anger on you. I'm saving it all for the K-King! (*Confidentially.*) And you know what?

PARROT: W-What? W-What?

TARTAGLIA: No one c-can save him b-because no one knows.

PARROT: No-one. No-one.

TARTAGLIA: You got it, my friend.

GENERAL SPAVENTO: (*Entering in a tizzy.*) My Lord Tartaglia, dinner is waiting, and King Deramo is calling for you!

TARTAGLIA: What?

GENERAL SPAVENTO: The King! Hurry!

TARTAGLIA: Of course. Mustn't k-keep a k-king waiting. May he eat as if it were his last meal on earth. I'm c-coming, G-General. After you.

GENERAL SPAVENTO: Oh, no. According to protocol, after YOU.

TARTAGLIA: (*Smiling sweetly.*) Oh, no. I insist.

GENERAL SPAVENTO: Why, thank you, old chap. That's very sporting of you. (*TARTAGLIA and GENERAL SPAVENTO exit.*)

PARROT: Amber-Forest. Amber-Forest. Dan-ger. Dan-ger. Dan-ger. (*LIGHTS.*)

*

SCENE 4

(The next morning. The street. Music. Enter PANTALONE with ANGELA, TARTAGLIA with CLARICE, and GENERAL SPAVENTO with SMERALDINA from their respective houses. The men are dressed for the hunt and carry rifles. Opening lines overlap.)

PANTALONE: Goodbye, Angela.
ANGELA: Good luck, Father.
GENERAL SPAVENTO: So long, Smeraldina.
SMERALDINA: Au revoir.
TARTAGLIA: Farewell, C-clarice.
CLARICE: Farewell.
ANGELA: Be careful, Father.
PANTALONE: Oh, yes. Don't worry.
GENERAL SPAVENTO: Be good, now.
SMERALDINA: What else?
TARTAGLIA: B-be sure to feed the d-dog.
CLARICE: I will. (*A TRUMPET is heard.*)
PANTALONE: Ah! The King!
GENERAL SPAVENTO: Stand back. Look sharp.
TARTAGLIA: Smile, C-clarice. (*KING DERAMO enters right with LEANDRO, both ready for the hunt.*)
KING DERAMO: Good morning, gentlemen. And ladies. (*A brief exchange of greetings.*)
GENERAL SPAVENTO: You're right on schedule, sire.
KING DERAMO: It's a beautiful day for the hunt. Let's waste no time, my friends. To the Amber Forest! (*KING DERAMO moves toward Angela.*) Angela, my dear. Rooms have been readied for you at the palace. You may spend the

night there if you wish to prepare for our wedding.

ANGELA: May I, Father?

PANTALONE: Certainly, child. It's traditional, after all.

ANGELA: May I bring Clarice? She's to be my Maid of Honor.

KING DERAMO: Of course. As long as Tartaglia agrees.

CLARICE: May I go, Brother?

TARTAGLIA: You m-may. But you must stay away from . . . (*Pointing to Leandro.*) . . . HIM! D-do I have your word on that?

CLARICE: Yes.

KING DERAMO: It's settled then. Come, my lords, there are bears and wolves and deer aplenty waiting for us in the forest! Farewell, Angela. I'll see you soon, my love. (*KING DERAMO exits with LEANDRO.*)

PANTALONE: Have a good time, my child.

ANGELA: Thank you, Father. (*PANTALONE exits.*)

GENERAL SPAVENTO: Cheerio! We're off! (*GENERAL SPAVENTO exits, followed by TARTAGLIA.*)

CLARICE: Oh, Angela! Won't this be fun? I'll just get my things and be down in a minute.

ANGELA: All right. I'll meet you here as soon as I've packed. (*CLARICE exits into her house. ANGELA starts to exit to hers.*)

SMERALDINA: (*Stopping Angela.*) Wouldn't like another bridesmaid, would you, Angela?

ANGELA: Of course, Smeraldina, I'd be delighted. Would you?

SMERALDINA: I'd be honored.

ANGELA: That will be wonderful.

SMERALDINA: See you at the palace then.

ANGELA: All right. (*ANGELA exits into her house.*)

SMERALDINA: I'll cry, of course. I always cry at a wedding. Mostly because it's not MY wedding. (*Enter TRUFFALDINO with a map and telescope. HE does not notice Smeraldina.*) Look who's here.

TRUFFALDINO: (*Trying to read the map.*) Let's see. "Town square. Old church. Monument to Deramo the First. Water works. Amusement park." (*Finding what he wants on the map.*) Ah, here we are. "B-3: Ancient Fortress on Sugarloaf Hill." B-3? Must be over there. (*As TRUFFALDINO, using his telescope, searches for the hill, SMERALDINA picks up an empty flower basket and strolls behind him.*) Well, I don't know. As fortresses go, that's the biggest mess I've ever seen. Unless . . . (*HE checks his map as SMERALDINA tries to get his attention.*) Ah-ha! Just as I thought, that's not B-3, it's C-4. (*Reads.*) "C-4: Ancient Junkyard." No wonder. So that means . . . the fortress must be over there. (*Raises telescope. SMERALDINA just happens to walk in front of it.*) Now, that . . . that doesn't look like any fortress I've ever seen either. In fact, it looks surprisingly like . . . a girl. (*Lowering telescope.*) Oh! It is. A girl. I mean, what'dya know? It's you!

SMERALDINA: Are you addressing me?

TRUFFALDINO: I'll say I am. I'm Truffaldino, remember?

SMERALDINA: Oh, yes. You're the one who fell in love with me yesterday, aren't you.

TRUFFALDINO: It's nice of you to remember. Say, I was sorry to hear about your bad luck.

SMERALDINA: I beg your pardon?

TRUFFALDINO: Well, you know. Not being chosen Queen.

SMERALDINA: Oh, that. That was of no concern to me.

I was actually relieved. Don't tell anyone I mentioned it, but the magician's statue told the King that I didn't really care for him.

TRUFFALDINO: No kidding.

SMERALDINA: I suppose I would have married him anyway, out of duty, but my heart wasn't in it.

TRUFFALDINO: Brave as well as beautiful! Golly! And where are you off to now?

SMERALDINA: I thought I might pick some flowers, over there, on Sugarloaf Hill.

TRUFFALDINO: What an amazing coincidence. That's just where I was going. May I join you?

SMERALDINA: Why not?

TRUFFALDINO: Here, allow me to carry your basket.

SMERALDINA: Why, thank you. You're a gentleman.

TRUFFALDINO: I'll carry you, too, if you like.

SMERALDINA: (*Giggles.*) I bet you couldn't.

TRUFFALDINO: (*Chuckles.*) I'll bet I could.

SMERALDINA: (*Giggles.*) I'd like to see you try.

TRUFFALDINO: (*Chuckles.*) You're going to see me try. (*TRUFFALDINO moves to her, starts to put basket down, freezes.*) What's that you've got in your basket?

SMERALDINA: What?

TRUFFALDINO: There's a piece of paper here. (*Reads.*) "Message from Norando to Truffaldino." Oh, here we go again. (*To Smeraldina.*) Excuse me a moment. It's for me. (*HE moves away.*)

SMERALDINA: What?

TRUFFALDINO: (*Reading.*) "The parrot has flown to the Amber Forest. Go there immediately and await further instructions."

SMERALDINA: What is going ON?

TRUFFALDINO: I'm afraid we have to postpone our walk, Smeraldina. This is a message from my master . . .

SMERALDINA: You expect me to believe that?

TRUFFALDINO: No, really. I've got to go to the Amber Forest to look for a parrot.

SMERALDINA: A parrot? Give me a break.

TRUFFALDINO: Do you think I'd make up something like that?

SMERALDINA: I wasn't born yesterday, Truffaldino. If you have other plans, why don't you just come right out and say so?

TRUFFALDINO: I don't have other plans, I just have to go now. See you later, Smeraldina.

SMERALDINA: (*To audience.*) I'm starting to feel just a tiny bit depressed. Losing out to Miss Goody-Two-Shoes-Angela is one thing. But a PARROT? Ooooh! (*SHE stamps her foot. Lights out.*)

*

SCENE 5

*(The Amber Forest. A lovely autumn day. From off up
left to off down right runs a brook—a narrow winding
strip of blue carpet. Left of center a small bridge spans
the brook. Up right center is a large boulder. As the
scene opens, THE PARROT is flapping his wings atop
the boulder, as if he had just landed.)*

PARROT: Am-ber. For-est. Am-ber. For-est. Dan-ger.
Dan-ger. Polly's here to watch it all. Awk! *(From offstage
are heard hunting horns and shouts. Enter KING DERAMO
with PANTALONE, TARTAGLIA, GENERAL SPAVENTO and
LEANDRO.)*
KING DERAMO: Well, my noble huntsmen, the skies are
clear and not a breeze is stirring. The forest will be filled with
game today. And, to add a bit of excitement to our sport, I'll
offer a bounty to the first man who brings down anything
bigger than a hare.
GENERAL SPAVENTO: A bounty, Your Majesty?
KING DERAMO: A prize of five hundred ducats to the
first true shot!
TARTAGLIA: A m-m-magnanimous offer.
LEANDRO: Thank you, Your Majesty.
GENERAL SPAVENTO: Capital! Splendid!
PANTALONE: Yes, sire, a generous and sporting
proposition . . .
GENERAL SPAVENTO: *(Interrupting, grandly.)* And
yet it's hardly fair, is it? What with my reputation as the
deadliest shot in the kingdom, you know . . .
PANTALONE: We know, General.
LEANDRO: We might get lucky.

GENERAL SPAVENTO: No, I insist. To even the odds, I shall shoot left-handed.

KING DERAMO: Very sporting of you, General.

TARTAGLIA: Perhaps we should divide our hunting party so we c-can c-cover more ground.

PANTALONE: Very well. How shall we proceed, gentlemen?

TARTAGLIA: One of us goes with the K-k-king, the other three hunt together.

KING DERAMO: All right. Who'll be my partner?

TARTAGLIA: Well, according to protocol . . .

PANTALONE: All right. We know. Tartaglia hunts with the King. Shall we get started?

GENERAL SPAVENTO: Come on, lads.

KING DERAMO: Good luck!

PANTALONE: If we make a kill, we'll signal with the hunting-horn. (*PANTALONE and LEANDRO move toward exit.*)

KING DERAMO: Good.

GENERAL SPAVENTO: (*To King Deramo.*) You know, sire, even left-handed, I'm afraid I've got 'em outclassed.

PANTALONE: Come on, General. You've got to shoot to win the bounty. Talking something to death doesn't count. (*PANTALONE exits with LEANDRO.*)

GENERAL SPAVENTO: (*As HE follows them off.*) Another of your jokes, I trust, my lord Pantalone. Very clever. (*KING DERAMO watches the departing figures, enjoying the banter.*)

TARTAGLIA: (*To audience.*) Now! If I c-can just get one c-clear shot at him while . . .

KING DERAMO: (*Turns to TARTAGLIA, who pretends to be polishing his gun.*) Well, Tartaglia, shall we take the opposite path? (*KING DERAMO moves past Tartaglia toward the opposite exit.*)

TARTAGLIA: Certainly, sire. (*KING DERAMO stops, surveying the view. TARTAGLIA addresses the audience.*) Now I'll be revenged. (*TARTAGLIA takes aim.*)

KING DERAMO: Such a beautiful spot, so calm and peaceful! (*Turns to face TARTAGLIA, who pretends to inspect his gun.*) Have you hunted here before, Tartaglia?

TARTAGLIA: No, Your Majesty. But I agree: it is beautiful. (*Pretends to see something in the distance.*) Look! Over there! (*KING DERAMO turns to look. TARTAGLIA aims, pulls trigger. The gun misfires. To audience.*) Ah, my gun's jammed! (*TARTAGLIA throws his gun down and kicks it.*) Blazes!

KING DERAMO: What's the matter, Tartaglia?

TARTAGLIA: (*Turning his back on Deramo.*) Agh! Now I'll have to find another way. C-curses!

KING DERAMO: What is it?

TARTAGLIA: It's nothing, sire. (*Getting a bright idea, HE wipes an imaginary tear from his eye.*) I'm only . . . a bit upset.

KING DERAMO: Upset? But, why, Tartaglia? What's troubling you?

TARTAGLIA: No, I'd rather not go into it.

KING DERAMO: Perhaps I can help you.

TARTAGLIA: No, believe me, it's nothing. (*TARTAGLIA stifles a sob.*)

KING DERAMO: Please! Tell me what has upset you.

TARTAGLIA: Well, Your Majesty, to speak frankly, I . . . no, no, never mind.

KING DERAMO: Tartaglia!

TARTAGLIA: Well . . . to speak frankly, Your Majesty,

it has been my dearest wish that someday I might win your trust.

KING DERAMO: I DO trust you, Tartaglia.

TARTAGLIA: No, Your Majesty, you do not!

KING DERAMO: I do!

TARTAGLIA: Do not! (*Sobs.*) I have certain proof. P-proof p-positive.

KING DERAMO: What on earth can you mean, Tartaglia? There is nothing I would not entrust to you.

TARTAGLIA: There is one thing. And you c-cannot deny it.   Yesterday you c-conferred in private with that magician . . .

KING DERAMO: Norando?

TARTAGLIA: Yes. And you admitted that he left two magical secrets in your hands. One of them—the secret of the statue—you explained to everyone. But the other secret you have kept hidden, even from me, your own Prime Minister. It is OBVIOUS that you do not trust me! (*Sobs.*)

KING DERAMO: Do not weep, my friend. It is true that I have kept the secret from you. Norando told me to guard it with my life. But you, the guardian of my life, my faithful Prime Minister and friend, shall share it with me. (*Produces from his pocket a black and gold card.*) Look, Tartaglia, with this verse, you can change your shape completely. Recite it over the body of any dead creature and you will instantly become that creature. Your own body will fall to the ground, lifeless and still.

TARTAGLIA: Perhaps Your Majesty is making a joke.

KING DERAMO: Don't you see? The charm is reversible. Once you have passed into the form of another creature, you may repeat the verse and return to your usual shape. With this amazing power, a man might easily disguise himself so as to detect every crime in our kingdom!

TARTAGLIA: (*Getting a brilliant idea.*) Or . . . a man might use the power to commit any crime.

KING DERAMO: Yes. It is a dangerous secret. That is why I have shared it with no one. But I present it as proof of my trust in you, Tartaglia.

TARTAGLIA: (*Moving away from Deramo with card. To audience.*) If this works, I will be rid of Deramo and reunited with Angela. (*To Deramo.*) Your Majesty. This is a generous sign of your faith. Forgive my doubts.

KING DERAMO: Say no more, Tartaglia. (*A GUN SHOT is heard from offstage.*)

TARTAGLIA: The hunters are c-coming this way. (*TARTAGLIA pockets the card just as a STAG enters, running.*)

KING DERAMO: Look at that, Tartaglia! A king stag! (*Rushes to get his gun and raises it as the STAG exits.*) Ah! He's out of range now. (*Enter PANTALONE, GENERAL SPAVENTO and LEANDRO.*)

GENERAL SPAVENTO: By Jove, he's wounded! I tell you, I hit him!

PANTALONE: No, General. (*Displaying a hole in his hat with a finger through it.*) What you wounded was my hat.

LEANDRO: Please, General. We all beg you: shoot right-handed!

PANTALONE: Did you see the stag, Your Majesty?

KING DERAMO: Yes. He ran that way.

LEANDRO: Let's go then. (*Exiting.*) The next shot is mine!

GENERAL SPAVENTO: All right, then. You asked for it! The next time I shoot . . . (*Exiting.*) I fire with this deadly right forefinger!

PANTALONE: (*Following them off.*) Just don't shoot

when I'm in front of you, that's all I ask. (*PANTALONE, GENERAL SPAVENTO and LEANDRO are gone.*)

KING DERAMO: Let's go, Tartaglia! I'll bet you're ready for a shot yourself.

TARTAGLIA: You took the words right out of my mouth, Your Majesty. (*GUNSHOTS from offstage are heard.*)

KING DERAMO: Tartaglia! The king stag! Take cover! (*KING DERAMO and TARTAGLIA withdraw.*) You take the first shot.

TARTAGLIA: I c-can't, Your Majesty. This blasted g-gun is j-jammed.

KING DERAMO: Then he's mine. Here he is! (*The STAG bounds onstage. KING DERAMO rises, gun in hand. The STAG rears, starts to run upstage. KING DERAMO fires. The STAG falls.*)

TARTAGLIA: (*Rising, moving first to Deramo, then to the stag.*) B-bravo! Good shot, Your Majesty! Looks like you just saved yourself five hundred ducats.

KING DERAMO: Thank you, Tartaglia. Let's call the others. I think the General deserves to hear ME do a little boasting for once. (*KING DERAMO raises his hunting horn.*)

TARTAGLIA: No, not yet, sire. Not yet!

KING DERAMO: Why not?

TARTAGLIA: Just think! What a perfect opportunity for testing the magic formula!

KING DERAMO: You mean, the stag?

TARTAGLIA: Precisely.

KING DERAMO: Why not? Go on, then. Give it a try.

TARTAGLIA: (*Chuckles nervously.*) Uh, let's see . . . (*Reading from the card.*) "Light, dark, d-d-dolphin, shark,
 Ca, ca, trif, c-c-c-ca . . ." It's no use, Your Majesty! I c-can't do it!

KING DERAMO: What's the matter?

TARTAGLIA: I'm so n-nervous, I c-can't c-control my s-stuttering. I c-can't get the words out.

KING DERAMO: Here, give me the verse. I'll try it.

TARTAGLIA: No, sire. It's too dangerous!

KING DERAMO: Nonsense! I'm not a bit afraid, I assure you.

TARTAGLIA: Oh, but you mustn't.

KING DERAMO: By heaven, I shall. Watch carefully, Tartaglia. All you have to do is place your right hand over the heart of the dead body and recite . . .

TARTAGLIA: Yes?

KING DERAMO: "Light, dark, dolphin shark, Ca ca trif, ca ca traf, Dry, wet, zenette!" (*KING DERAMO's body stiffens. The STAG's body trembles. KING DERAMO's body slowly falls while the STAG raises his head, then starts to rise.*)

TARTAGLIA: (*To audience.*) Good heavens! It DID work! (*To the Stag.*) It did work, didn't it, Your Majesty?

STAG-DERAMO: (*With a laugh.*) You see, Tartaglia. King Deramo now exists in the body of the King Stag.

TARTAGLIA: Fantastic! (*Picking up the card on which the verse is written.*) With this charm, a man might d-do anything. Anything in the world!

STAG-DERAMO: (*Rising, somewhat slowly and painfully.*) Yes. Disguised in many shapes, a king might root out all wrongs in his realm.

TARTAGLIA: (*Petting the stag's head.*) Yes, Your Majesty. OR, another man might . . . (*Picking up Deramo's gun.*) . . . disguise himself as a k-k-king and enjoy the royal powers, the royal treasury, or even the royal bride.

STAG-DERAMO: Don't joke about a thing like that, Tartaglia. I'll return to my body now. (*Placing hoof on*

Deramo's body.) How does the verse begin? "Light, dark, dolphin, shark . . ." What comes next?

TARTAGLIA: What comes next, Your Majesty, is a gun shot. I'm about to bag myself a king stag, and the next verse you hear will b-be your epitaph.

STAG-DERAMO: No! Don't! (*The STAG runs off. TARTAGLIA squeezes the trigger, but the gun does not fire.*)

TARTAGLIA: D-drat! The thing's not even loaded! Agh! I mustn't let him get away! (*TARTAGLIA starts off, then stops.*) Wait a minute! I'd better make the most of my opportunity first. (*Moves to Deramo's body, placing his hand upon it.*) "Light, dark, dolphin shark, C-ca c-ca trif, c-ca c-ca traf . . ." C-curse that c-clumsy stammer of mine! "Dry, wet, zenette!"   (*The same transfer business occurs. TARTAGLIA's body falls; KING DERAMO's rises.*)

KING DERAMO-TARTAGLIA: So b-be it! Long live K-k-king Tartaglia! All I must do now is kill the stag; and the c-crown, the k-kingdom and Angela are mine! (*Blows the HUNTING HORN.*) Hunters! C-come back! Oops! I nearly forgot. I'd better hide this. (*HE drags TARTAGLIA's body out of sight as HUNTING HORNS are heard offstage.*)

PANTALONE: (*Offstage.*) Coming, Your Majesty!

LEANDRO: (*Offstage.*) Someone must have shot the stag.

GENERAL SPAVENTO: (*Offstage.*) Pure luck, no doubt.

PANTALONE: (*As HE enters with LEANDRO and GENERAL SPAVENTO.*) Yes, Your Majesty? Have you killed the stag, sire?

KING DERAMO-TARTAGLIA: No, you idiot! B-but he must be killed at once! (*Points off.*) He went that way. After him! Fire at will! (*THEY ALL rush off, DERAMO-TARTAGLIA leading the way.*)

GENERAL SPAVENTO: (*Offstage.*) My shot, my shot! Where is he?

LEANDRO: (*Offstage.*) There! (*GUNSHOTS are heard. The STAG runs back on and stops suddenly, freezing. Enter an OLD HERMIT, not seeing the stag. THE STAG sneaks off. Meanwhile, we have been hearing from offstage . . .*)

PANTALONE: (*Offstage.*)   You missed him, too, Leandro.

LEANDRO: (*Offstage.*) He's too fast for us!

GENERAL SPAVENTO: (*Offstage.*) I won't miss next time.

KING DERAMO-TARTAGLIA: Whoever misses next time will pay for it! C-c-come on! He went this way. Hurry! (*Enter PANTALONE, GENERAL SPAVENTO, DERAMO-TARTAGLIA and LEANDRO, just after the exit of the STAG but while the OLD HERMIT is still crossing the stage.*)

LEANDRO: He doubled back this way.

KING DERAMO-TARTAGLIA: Are you sure?

LEANDRO: Positive.

KING DERAMO-TARTAGLIA: C-curses! No sign of him. (*To the Old Hermit.*) You there!

OLD HERMIT: Me?

KING DERAMO-TARTAGLIA: Yes, you! Which way did the stag run?

OLD HERMIT: Stag?

KING DERAMO-TARTAGLIA: The one that just ran through here.

OLD HERMIT: A stag?

KING DERAMO-TARTAGLIA: (*Furious.*) Yes! A king stag!

OLD HERMIT: Well, what do you know.

KING DERAMO-TARTAGLIA: Are you deaf? Speak

up! Where is that stag?

OLD HERMIT: I saw no stag.

KING DERAMO-TARTAGLIA: (*In a great rage.*) SAW NO STAG! (*Hits the Old Hermit with his gun.*) You doddering old fossil! (*Turns abruptly to the others.*) Kill him!

OLD HERMIT: No, no . . .

PANTALONE: Excuse me, Your Majesty?

KING DERAMO-TARTAGLIA: Shoot him.

OLD HERMIT: (*Backing away slowly.*) Please . . .

PANTALONE: But why, Your Majesty?

KING DERAMO-TARTAGLIA: Cowards! (*Rips gun out of Pantalone's hands.*) Here's medicine for your cough, old man. (*Shoots. The OLD HERMIT gasps and falls dead. The OTHERS watch, frozen with horror. A pause.*) Stand back, all of you! (*Points the gun at them.*) Do not annoy me, gentlemen. As you c-can see, I'm not in the mood to be c-contradicted. From now on, speak only when I bid you to do so. Is that c-c-clear? (*PANTALONE, GENERAL SPAVENTO and LEANDRO respond simultaneously.*)

GENERAL SPAVENTO: Quite.

PANTALONE: Of course.

LEANDRO: Certainly.

KING DERAMO-TARTAGLIA: Good. Well, as the sun has almost set, it is too late to c-continue the hunt today. But tomorrow, at the c-crack of dawn, I want a d-dozen marksmen here to track the k-king stag. I'll pay a thousand ducats to the man who shoots him. (*Eyeing them suspiciously.*) Why, you ask?

PANTALONE: I beg your pardon, Your Majesty?

KING DERAMO-TARTAGLIA: I said, you're asking WHY I want the stag killed at any c-cost.

GENERAL SPAVENTO: Oh, yes, indeed! We're asking!

(*Weakly.*) Why?

KING DERAMO-TARTAGLIA: Because I am determined to make a present of him to my b-bride-to-b-be, Angela.

PANTALONE: (*Lip service.*) Very thoughtful, sire.

GENERAL SPAVENTO: Yes, a lovely sentiment, I must . . .

KING DERAMO-TARTAGLIA: Silence! Now I shall return to the palace—my palace. My throne, my crown, my darling Angela.

GENERAL SPAVENTO: Certainly, sire. (*ALL start to move toward exit.*)

PANTALONE: But what about the Prime Minister, sire?

LEANDRO: That's right. Where is Tartaglia?

KING DERAMO-TARTAGLIA: (*Stopping suddenly.*) WHERE? (*Laughs.*) Yes, where is my beloved Prime Minister?

PANTALONE: The last time I saw him he was with you, sire.

KING DERAMO-TARTAGLIA: No, we separated when the stag was sighted. Have none of you seen him since?

PANTALONE: Not I, sire.

LEANDRO : Not I.

GENERAL SPAVENTO: Nor I.

KING DERAMO-TARTAGLIA: Hmm. I suspect foul play.

LEANDRO: But why, Your Majesty? He probably fell behind during the chase and decided to return to the city.

KING DERAMO-TARTAGLIA: Perhaps. On the other hand, someone . . . (*Looking them over maliciously.*) . . . might have murdered him. I know how he was hated because he was the K-King's, I mean, MY favorite minister. If he has not returned to the palace by nightfall, I shall c-conduct a thorough investigation. C-c-come now. Follow me! (*DERAMO-TARTAGLIA exits. The OTHERS remain behind, frozen with astonishment.*)

PANTALONE: (*After a beat.*) I never noticed that stutter of his before.

GENERAL SPAVENTO: Reminds me of someone, but I can't think who. (*Looking at the fallen Hermit.*) Poor beggar. Ugh!

LEANDRO: Well, what do we do now?

PANTALONE: What else can we do? (*As HE exits.*) We must follow the King. (*The OTHERS follow PANTALONE out as the STAG-DERAMO enters cautiously.*)

STAG-KING DERAMO: (*Breathing hard and speaking with difficulty.*) So hard. To use. The body of this stag. So hard. To think clearly. But I must find some way to stop Tartaglia. (*Sees Hermit's body on the ground.*) What's this? Old man! Wake up! It's not safe to sleep here. You must get up . . . (*Stops short.*) He's dead! Good heavens! What could've happened that he should have been left here without so much as a friend to bury him? Well, poor soul, perhaps I can at least drag you into the thicket . . . (*Starts to move the Hermit. Stops short.*) Wait a minute! If I use the body of this man, instead of the stag's, I shall be able to return to the palace. If only I can remember the charm. (*Placing a hoof on the Hermit's chest.*) "Light, dark, dolphin, shark . . ." What's next? "Ca, ca, trif, ca, ca traf, Dry, wet . . .zenette!" (*Transfer business again occurs. The STAG falls. The HERMIT rises.*)

OLD HERMIT-KING DERAMO: Ah! My good stars have not deserted me. I am the King again! (*Starting off, HE falters, clutching his head.*) Ah! I feel so weak! (*HE moves to the brook.*) I must clear my head. (*As HE leans over the*

brook to dab water to his forehead, HE freezes in horror.)
Agh! (*HE looks again, testing the image.*) No! I am Deramo!
I am the King! (*Sinks back wearily, staring into space.*) What
am I to do? Who will believe me? Angela! My precious
bride! Tonight she will be greeted by Tartaglia—by Tartaglia
within my body. Will she know? (*Struggles to his knees.*)
Hear me, Angela! You MUST know! (*His strength leaves
him once again. HE looks wearily back at the stag.*) What has
happened here is evil. And I, weak and ill, trapped in this old
man's body, I must find the way to overcome Tartaglia.
Tartaglia! Monster! Your battle is not won yet. Deramo is
coming. (*The OLD HERMIT-KING DERAMO starts to exit.
Before he is gone, TRUFFALDINO enters with his telescope,
whistling cheerfully.*) Truffaldino!

TRUFFALDINO: (*After looking behind himself, thinking
the Old Hermit-King Deramo might be addressing someone
else.*) Have we met?

OLD HERMIT-KING DERAMO: I must find Norando.

TRUFFALDINO: No kidding.

OLD HERMIT-KING DERAMO: Truffaldino! Where is
Norando?

TRUFFALDINO: No telling. Disappeared. Happens all
the time.

OLD HERMIT-KING DERAMO: Disappeared!

TRUFFALDINO: Say, who ARE you, anyway?

OLD HERMIT-KING DERAMO: I'm . . . Never mind.
I must hurry. (*Starts out.*) If you should meet Norando, tell
him that I . . . tell him to come to the palace. Tell him that
Deramo needs his help! (*HE exits.*)

TRUFFALDINO: Sure thing. (*Shouting off after Old
Hermit-King Deramo.*) I don't know when I'll see him,
though. I've got to wait around for a parrot.

PARROT: (*Still on boulder.*) Here-I-am. Here-I-am.

TRUFFALDINO: Did   I   hear   something? (*TRUFFALDINO looks through his telescope.*)

PARROT: Over-here. Over-here.

TRUFFALDINO: I bet that parrot is around here somewhere. (*Starts to tiptoe around boulder.*)

PARROT: Some-where. Some-where.

TRUFFALDINO: That's what I said. Somewhere. But where? (*Disappears behind boulder, calling.*) Pol-ly! Good Polly. Pretty Polly. Where are you, you nut head?

PARROT: Polly-here. Polly-here. Awk! (*The parrot's wings flap as it disappears behind the boulder.*)

TRUFFALDINO: (*Out of sight.*) Come out, come out, wherever you are. Come on, Polly! (*HE reappears. The parrot, a note in its beak, is sitting on TRUFFALDINO's hand. HE sighs in disgust.*) This could take all day. There are three million places that parrot could be in this forest. I don't even know where to begin. (*TRUFFALDINO, using the hand on which the parrot sits, scratches his head.*) Meanwhile, who knows what Smeraldina's up to while I'm out here bird-watching. (*HE holds up his telescope and looks through it. The parrot is directly in front of him.*) Not to mention the fact that it'll be getting dark pretty soon. And what about my dinner? If that bird comes between me and my dinner, it's going to be war. (*HE starts to place the hand on which the parrot sits under his chin. HE sees the parrot at last and shrieks.*) WHAT'S THE STORY, Pol? I've been looking for you everywhere.

PARROT: Polly-here. Polly-here.

TRUFFALDINO: No-kidding. No-kidding.

PARROT: Awk!

TRUFFALDINO: What's this? (*Taking note from parrot's*

beak.) You're a regular carrier pigeon, aren't you.

PARROT: (*Angrily.*) Awk!

TRUFFALDINO: All right, don't get excited. (*Reads.*) "Norando to Truffaldino." (*To audience.*) I don't know about you, but I'm practically struck dumb with surprise. (*Reads.*) "Take parrot back to palace. Tell the King that you have killed the king stag." (*Looks at stag's body, shudders dramatically. To audience.*) I just can't stand the sight of blood. (*Reads.*) "Further instructions will follow." (*To audience.*) I was afraid of that. (*To Parrot.*) All right, Pol. We've got our marching orders. Ready to rock and roll?

PARROT: Read-y. Read-y. (*THEY start out.*)

TRUFFALDINO: All RIGHT! Say, did you hear about the human cannonball at the circus?

PARROT: No-no.

TRUFFALDINO: He got fired. (*TRUFFALDINO laughs wildly as HE and Parrot exit.*)

*

SCENE 6

(The street. Early evening. Enter PANTALONE, LEANDRO and GENERAL SPAVENTO, from the hunt. THEY look weary and dispirited. The TRIO halts at left center and heaves a huge, unanimous sigh.)

PANTALONE: Well . . .

GENERAL SPAVENTO: Well . . .

LEANDRO: Well . . .

PANTALONE: Here we are.

GENERAL SPAVENTO: (*Adopting a positive approach.*) Yes, indeed. Home again. Home again. Jiggity-jig. (*Pause.*)

LEANDRO: What are we going to do?

GENERAL SPAVENTO: Do?

LEANDRO: About the King.

GENERAL SPAVENTO: Aha! That is the question.

PANTALONE: Exactly. (*Pause.*) Well. Now we know the question. What is the answer?

LEANDRO: We've got to do something! Are you forgetting that Angela and Clarice are in the palace at this very moment?

PANTALONE: Oh, my heavens!

LEANDRO: If the King is half as crazy as he was this afternoon, who knows what will happen?

PANTALONE: You're right, Leandro. If only we knew what to do!

GENERAL SPAVENTO: Oh, come now. That's a rather pessimistic view, I must say. Why don't you look on the bright side?

LEANDRO: The what side?

GENERAL SPAVENTO: The, uh, you know, bright side.

LEANDRO: Perhaps it's slipped your mind, General. This afternoon King Deramo killed an innocent man in cold blood. For all we know, he's done away with Tartaglia, too. Where's the bright side to that? Eh? Are you on the moon, or what?

GENERAL SPAVENTO: I really don't care for your tone of voice, old boy. I simply meant that there might be some perfectly logical explanation for the King's behavior today. Let's not jump to conclusions, after all. Haste makes waste and all that, you know.

LEANDRO: Indeed? Well, that's ever so helpful. "Haste makes waste." What about "Don't count your chickens before they've hatched?" My God! Why didn't I think of that?

PANTALONE: Hold on, Leandro. All right, General, let's hear your "perfectly logical explanation" for the King's behavior today.

GENERAL SPAVENTO: Well . . .

LEANDRO: Well?

GENERAL SPAVENTO: He may simply have had a splitting headache. (*There is a pause.*)

PANTALONE: I'm getting a headache. I'm getting a really bad headache.

GENERAL SPAVENTO: He may have had a touch of spotted fever. Makes him a bit peculiar today, but tomorrow . . . (*Snaps his fingers.*) . . . it's gone!

LEANDRO: Tomorrow we may all be gone.

GENERAL SPAVENTO: Or . . . To look on the really bright side, perhaps he's gotten lost in the forest or, uh . . . or, uh . . . You could be right. Maybe there IS no bright side.

PANTALONE: Thank you, General. A penetrating analysis.

GENERAL SPAVENTO: Anytime, old chap. The

military mind, you know.

LEANDRO: May I suggest a plan?

PANTALONE: Please do.   I'm worried sick about Angela.

LEANDRO: There's no alternative. We've got to get rid of Deramo.

PANTALONE: You mean . . . ?

LEANDRO: Yes. Depose him.

PANTALONE: Overthrow the King!

GENERAL SPAVENTO: Of course! Kick him off the throne. Leandro, my lad, you're a genius!

PANTALONE: But General . . .

GENERAL SPAVENTO: Yes?

PANTALONE: That's treason.

GENERAL SPAVENTO: By Jove, it IS treason, isn't it? Leandro, my lad, you're a traitor. I'm terribly sorry, old boy, but I'm afraid I must arrest you.

LEANDRO: All right! It's treason. Who cares what it's called? We can't have a madman on the throne.

PANTALONE: (*To the General.*) Perhaps he's right. (*To Leandro.*) But how could it be done?

LEANDRO: Perhaps I can persuade the Palace Guards to side with us. If so, we need only arrest Deramo and send him into exile.

PANTALONE: Very well. I'll go along with you, but only if you let me speak to the King first. He deserves a chance to explain himself.

LEANDRO: That will only make it more dangerous for us.

PANTALONE: Nevertheless, that's my condition. Otherwise I'll have no part of it.

GENERAL SPAVENTO: Right. Fair play and all that.

LEANDRO: All right. Now we mustn't lose any more time. Let's go.

GENERAL SPAVENTO: Where?

LEANDRO: To the palace.

GENERAL SPAVENTO: Now?

LEANDRO: At once.

GENERAL SPAVENTO: No, no, no. Strategy, my boy, that's what wanted. Cautious formulation of a foolproof plan. Consider the odds, the enemy's strength, the lay of the land . . .

PANTALONE: We're leaving now, General. Unless you're afraid . . .

GENERAL SPAVENTO: Afraid? General Spavento laughs at fear. (*HE produces a weak, cracked laugh.*) Ha-ha-ha.

LEANDRO: Well, there are three of us. It's not much of a chance, but it's the only one we have. Let's hurry. (*LEANDRO and PANTALONE exit.*)

GENERAL SPAVENTO: Let me try that again. Ha-ha-ha. That's it. Here we go. Chin up. Stiff upper. For-ward march! One-two, one-two! (*HE exits at double-time.*)

*

SCENE 7

(The palace gardens. Evening. Strings of decorative lanterns burn brightly. At left of center stands a dress-maker's mannequin wearing Angela's wedding gown. SMERALDINA, on her knees, stitches the hem, while CLARICE works on a sleeve. At the table, right, ANGELA works with needle and thread on her headdress and veil. Beside her lies a hand mirror. [Note: a breakaway replica has replaced the actor playing the Statue.])

ANGELA: And then he said, "In my excitement I forgot to say . . . I love you, Angela."

CLARICE & SMERALDINA: *(In unison.)* Awwwwwwwwww . . .

ANGELA: And then he said that it was the happiest day of his life!

CLARICE & SMERALDINA: *(In unison.)* Awwwwwwwwwwwww . . .

SMERALDINA: Ouch!

CLARICE: Uh-oh.

SMERALDINA: Oooo! Stuck my finger!

ANGELA: It's gotten too dark to go on sewing, Smeraldina. We'll finish it tomorrow.

SMERALDINA: No, I'm almost done.

CLARICE: Isn't it beautiful, Angela?

ANGELA: Oh, yes, Clarice!

SMERALDINA: There! *(Breaking thread with her teeth.)* Ta-tum! *(Rises.)* The Royal Wedding Gown!

CLARICE: *(Curtsying.)* Fit for a queen, Your Highness.

SMERALDINA: *(Curtsying.)* Does it please your Royal

Highness?

ANGELA: (*Embracing them in turn.*) Oh, yes! Thank you. Both of you. (*THEY examine the gown from various angles.*) Do you think the King will like it?

SMERALDINA: If he notices it.

CLARICE: As long as you're wearing it, Angela, the King will be enchanted.

SMERALDINA: Ah, yes! Love, love, love! Tsk, tsk, tsk. Poor Angela!

ANGELA: (*Laughs.*) What do you mean, Smeraldina?

SMERALDINA: Well, you know what they say: the joys of love last but a day.

CLARICE: Not in the case of King Deramo, I'm sure.

ANGELA: Oh, I'm sure of that, too. Yesterday he said that he would love me "as long as flowers bloom and stars still shine."

CLARICE: How beautiful! How romantic!

SMERALDINA: They all say that. Today it's . . . (*Uses mannequin.*) . . . "Your lips like rare red wine, the scent of jasmine in your hair, the glint of starlight in your eyes . . ." Tomorrow: (*Shoves the mannequin about as CLARICE and ANGELA scramble to prevent its toppling over.*) "Clean the house, dinner at eight, I'm off to hunt with the boys, don't wait up."

CLARICE: Don't be silly, Smeraldina. The King would never treat Angela that way.

SMERALDINA: They're all the same.

ANGELA: Not Deramo.

CLARICE: He's kind . . .

ANGELA: He's sweet . . .

SMERALDINA: He's young. Just wait.

CLARICE: He's gentle. . .

ANGELA: He's shy . . .

SMERALDINA: He's . . .

A GUARD: (*Entering.*) My lady, the King has returned from the hunt.

SMERALDINA: . . . he's here.

CLARICE: (*As THEY arrange themselves to greet the King.*) Now, Smeraldina, you'll see how tenderly the King treats Angela.

SMERALDINA: Oh, lighten up, Clarice. (*Enter KING DERAMO-TARTAGLIA.*) Good evening, sire.

CLARICE: (*Curtsying.*) Your Majesty.

ANGELA: Welcome home, my King.

KING DERAMO-TARTAGLIA: (*Brusquely, to Clarice and Smeraldina.*) You two. Out!

SMERALDINA: I beg your pardon, sire?

KING DERAMO-TARTAGLIA: Out. Q-quick!

SMERALDINA: Oh. All right. (*SHE starts out.*)

CLARICE: Certainly, Your Majesty. (*SHE starts out.*)

KING DERAMO-TARTAGLIA: C-clarice!

CLARICE: Yes, sire?

KING DERAMO-TARTAGLIA: K-keep away from that Leandro, understand?

CLARICE: (*Puzzled.*) Yes, sire.

SMERALDINA: (*To Clarice.*) Shy and gentle, isn't he.

KING DERAMO-TARTAGLIA: Out! (*SMERALDINA and CLARICE exit.*) Now. Angela! Beautiful Angela. C-come here, d-dear.

ANGELA: (*Approaching him.*) Was your luck good, my lord?

KING DERAMO-TARTAGLIA: Luck?

ANGELA: In the hunt.

KING DERAMO-TARTAGLIA: (*Chuckling.*) The b-best

of luck. And now . . . (*Taking her hand.*) . . . this hand is mine! (*Kisses her hand roughly.*) Angela is m-mine! Aren't you, my d-dear?

ANGELA: Your Majesty . . .

KING DERAMO-TARTAGLIA: Hm?

ANGELA: You're hurting my hand.

KING DERAMO-TARTAGLIA: Ah. Let me see it. So small and d-delicate. Must remember always to be gentle with this t-tiny little hand. (*Kisses it gently.*) Angela, my sweet, d-do you love me?

ANGELA: (*Teasingly.*) Do you think my love lasts only one day?

KING DERAMO-TARTAGLIA: Tell me. T-tell me you love me!

ANGELA: I . . . love you. (*KING DERAMO-TARTAGLIA chuckles.*) Is something wrong, sire?

KING DERAMO-TARTAGLIA: Why, no. Everything is right at last.

ANGELA: I meant . . . do you feel quite well?

KING DERAMO-TARTAGLIA: Tartaglia never felt b-better in his life!

ANGELA: Tartaglia?

KING DERAMO-TARTAGLIA: Uh. Yes. That's what he told me just this afternoon. I . . . too, have never been in better health. (*Trying to plant his new identity in his mind, pounding on every hard surface available.*) I . . . King Deramo! Deramo . . . D-deramo . . . King Deramo!

ANGELA: (*Watching him with growing concern.*) What is it, sire?

KING DERAMO-TARTAGLIA: What's what?

ANGELA: You don't seem to be yourself this evening.

KING DERAMO-TARTAGLIA: Don't be ridiculous.

There's nothing wrong with King Deramo that a k-kiss won't c-cure. Come here, my dear. Give me a little k-kiss. (*SHE hesitates*.) C-come here, I said. I c-command you! (*ANGELA approaches in a state of some confusion. As KING DERAMO-TARTAGLIA roughly embraces her, the GUARD enters*.)

GUARD: Your Majesty . . .

KING DERAMO-TARTAGLIA: G-go away. I'm busy!

GUARD: But, sire, there's a fellow here who says . . .

KING DERAMO-TARTAGLIA: No messages. I want to be alone with my b-b-bride-to-b-be.

GUARD: But, sire, he said he's found the stag.

KING DERAMO-TARTAGLIA: (*Big take.*) Stag? The k-king stag?

GUARD: Yes, sire.

KING DERAMO-TARTAGLIA: Send him in at once! (*The GUARD exits.*) Angela, my dear, we'll save the k-kiss until we hear my good news. (*Enter TRUFFALDINO, with the PARROT.*) You! Is it true you've found the stag?

TRUFFALDINO: Yes, Your Royal Holiness. Found him in the forest beside the brook.

KING DERAMO-TARTAGLIA: A k-king stag? White markings on the head? Gigantic antlers?

TRUFFALDINO: That's the one.

KING DERAMO-TARTAGLIA: Where is he now?

TRUFFALDINO: At the palace gates.

KING DERAMO-TARTAGLIA: D-dead or . . . alive?

TRUFFALDINO: Dead, Your Majesty.

KING DERAMO-TARTAGLIA: Ah-ha! (*To Angela.*) The king stag is dead, long live the King!

TRUFFALDINO: (*Placing the parrot in the niche.*) Take a seat, Polly.

KING DERAMO-TARTAGLIA: Show me the stag!

TRUFFALDINO: Yes, sir. (*TRUFFALDINO and KING DERAMO-TARTAGLIA start to exit.*) Oh! By the way . . . (*TRUFFALDINO halts.*) I hear there's a reward of a thousand ducats.

KING DERAMO-TARTAGLIA: (*Suspiciously.*) Well?

TRUFFALDINO: Well, it's mine, isn't it?

KING DERAMO-TARTAGLIA: (*Going along, pleasantly.*) So. You think a king like me should pay a thousand hard-earned ducats to a m-mere magician's flunky like you?

TRUFFALDINO: Sounds good to me. After all, I'm only asking for what I deserve.

KING DERAMO-TARTAGLIA: Guard! (*To Truffaldino.*) Oh, you'll g-get what you deserve.

TRUFFALDINO: Thank you, sire. When? (*Enter the GUARD.*)

KING DERAMO-TARTAGLIA: Now. Guard, throw this man into the d-d-dungeon!

TRUFFALDINO: (*Panics. Grabs King Deramo-Tartaglia. Nose to nose.*) D-d-dungeon?

KING DERAMO-TARTAGLIA: Are you m-mocking m-me?

TRUFFALDINO: M-mocking?

KING DERAMO-TARTAGLIA: With that st-stammer!

TRUFFALDINO: Oh, no, sire. You don't stammer. The one who stammers is Tartaglia.

KING DERAMO-TARTAGLIA: (*Throwing Truffaldino to the Guard.*) Ugh! I want him b-b-beheaded at dawn!

TRUFFALDINO: D-d-dawn?

KING DERAMO-TARTAGLIA: D-d-d . . . Make it noon!

TRUFFALDINO: Wait! Did you say b-b-beheaded?

KING DERAMO-TARTAGLIA: B-b-b . . . Hang him!

TRUFFALDINO: (*Holds Guard back. Composes himself a bit.*) Do you mind if I ask why?

KING DERAMO-TARTAGLIA: For the murder of my beloved Prime Minister, Tartaglia!

TRUFFALDINO: But that's ridiculous!

KING DERAMO-TARTAGLIA: Silence! Take him away!

GUARD: (*Clasping Truffaldino by the shoulder.*) Still think it's ridiculous?

TRUFFALDINO: It's ridiculous, all right, but it's not too funny.

KING DERAMO-TARTAGLIA: Get him out of here! (*A note pops out of the Guard's hat.*)

TRUFFALDINO: Look! A message from Norando! I'm sure this will explain everything. (*Reads.*) "Go to the dungeon. Go directly to the dungeon. Do not collect one thousand ducats. Do not worry." Do not worry?

KING DERAMO-TARTAGLIA: Take him away!

TRUFFALDINO: (*As he is led away.*) Sure, that explains everything. (*To the Guard.*) You heard what it said: do not worry. Look at me. Am I worrying? (*To himself.*) Do not worry, do not worry, do not worry . . .

ANGELA: Your Majesty, is it true that that boy killed Tartaglia?

KING DERAMO-TARTAGLIA: I saw it with my own eyes. (*Starts for door.*) Wait for me here, Angela. I must examine the stag. Then we shall celebrate! (*Stops, blows her a kiss.*) I won't b-be long, my love. (*Exits.*)

ANGELA: (*Alone.*) How extraordinary. He's like a completely different man. Perhaps he's ill. (*OLD HERMIT-KING DERAMO appears, climbing laboriously over the wall.*)

When he looked at me, it was as if he saw someone else. Have I changed, too? (*Moving to table and picking up mirror.*) What did he see? (*SHE looks at herself in the mirror, as OLD HERMIT-KING DERAMO moves weakly to her. SHE catches sight of something behind her in the mirror.*) Who's there? (*ANGELA turns, sees Old Hermit-King Deramo, gasps in fear. BOTH freeze for a moment.*)

OLD HERMIT-KING DERAMO: I'm sorry. Did I frighten you?

ANGELA: Only for a moment. What are you doing here?

OLD HERMIT-KING DERAMO: (*HE has difficulty getting his breath.*) I came . . . to see you.

ANGELA: Me?

OLD HERMIT-KING DERAMO: (*Ready to collapse.*) Yes. I came a long way, or so it seems. May I . . . sit down? (*HE nearly falls.*)

ANGELA: (*Rushing to help him to bench at center.*) Of course. You must rest. I'll send for a doctor. (*SHE starts out.*)

OLD HERMIT-KING DERAMO: No! I must speak to you!

ANGELA: Let the doctor see you first.

OLD HERMIT-KING DERAMO: Angela! (*SHE stops and looks at him strangely.*) Listen to me. Something terrible has happened. You are the only one who can help me.

ANGELA: (*Approaching him again cautiously.*) What is it? What do you want?

OLD HERMIT-KING DERAMO: What I will tell you is hard to believe. But if you CAN believe it, you must tell your father.

ANGELA: (*Sitting beside him.*) Go on.

OLD HERMIT-KING DERAMO: First the statue. Do you remember? The statue will smile at any lie.

ANGELA: How did you know that?

OLD HERMIT-KING DERAMO: I'll explain in just a moment . But quickly! Pass your hand over the statue's eyes. (*SHE does so*.) Watch the statue carefully as you listen to me. This is the truth: as strange as it seems, I am . . . (*Enter KING DERAMO-TARTAGLIA*.)

KING DERAMO-TARTAGLIA: Angela!

ANGELA: (*Gasping in surprise as SHE turns*.) Oh! Your Majesty! (*Laughs*.) Everything seems to startle me today. (*OLD HERMIT-KING DERAMO draws back, trying to cover his face*.)

KING DERAMO-TARTAGLIA: What do you mean?

ANGELA: This old man . . . (*OLD HERMIT-KING DERAMO keeps his face averted*.) . . . gave me a start just now. But he's perfectly harmless. He says . . .

OLD HERMIT-KING DERAMO: Not now, child. Perhaps I'll see you later.

KING DERAMO-TARTAGLIA: What are you doing here?

OLD HERMIT-KING DERAMO: (*Moving past King Deramo-Tartaglia*.) I came to wish this lady happiness in her marriage. I'll be going now.

KING DERAMO-TARTAGLIA: Be quick about it. And don't ever come into this p-palace without my p-permission again!

OLD HERMIT-KING DERAMO: Yes, sire. (*HE exits*.)

KING DERAMO-TARTAGLIA: Now, Angela . . . (*HE stops himself*.) Funny. It seems to me I've seen that face somewhere before. (*Tremendous "take"*.) The old hermit in the forest! (*Runs to the door and calls*.) Stop! Guards! B-bring that old man back to me immediately!

ANGELA: What is it, sire? What has he done?

KING DERAMO-TARTAGLIA: K-keep quiet! I'll handle this.   (*Enter two GUARDS with OLD HERMIT-KING DERAMO*.)

GUARD: Here he is, Your Majesty.

KING DERAMO-TARTAGLIA: Gag him! And bind his hands! (*The GUARDS do so quickly*.)

ANGELA: But, sire! Please don't let them hurt him. He's old and weak.

KING DERAMO-TARTAGLIA: Quiet! I knew I'd seen this old devil before. He's a d-dangerous lunatic. (*To the Guards*.) Leave him to me. (*As THEY hesitate*.) Well? What are you waiting for? Out! (*Exit the GUARDS*.)

ANGELA: (*Moving to Old Hermit-King Deramo*.) They've bound him too tightly!

KING DERAMO-TARTAGLIA: Angela, k-keep away from him! (*Pushing her away*.) I told you: he's dangerous.

ANGELA: I can't believe that.

KING DERAMO-TARTAGLIA: Would you doubt your King? (*Turns to Old Hermit-King Deramo, savoring his power*.) The game is over now. I win. You lose.

GUARD: (*Entering*.) Your Majesty . . .

KING DERAMO-TARTAGLIA: I told you to go!

GUARD: But your ministers, sire, and the Lieutenant of the Guards . . .

KING DERAMO-TARTAGLIA: I c-can't see anyone!

GUARD: They insist on being announced, Your Majesty . . .   (*Enter PANTALONE, GENERAL SPAVENTO, LEANDRO, CLARICE and SMERALDINA*.)

KING DERAMO-TARTAGLIA: (*Shoving Old Hermit-King Deramo out of sight behind the mannequin*.) Out of sight, you!

PANTALONE: (*After a short frozen silence*.) Your

Majesty . . .

GENERAL SPAVENTO: Terribly sorry to intrude, realize it's frightfully late and all that . . .

KING DERAMO-TARTAGLIA: (*After a brief pause, as GENERAL SPAVENTO runs out of gas.*) Well, I'm w-waiting, General. What do you w-want?

GENERAL SPAVENTO: (*Stepping forward reluctantly.*) Well, I . . . In fact, we . . . that is, they . . . thought you might . . . be feeling a bit under the weather. So we just dropped in to say . . . hope you're feeling better soon. And so forth.

KING DERAMO-TARTAGLIA: I see. Very c-considerate. (*GENERAL SPAVENTO buries himself in the ranks.*) Anything else?

PANTALONE: (*Stepping forward.*) Yes, sire. The fact is, we were hoping that you might be able to offer an explanation for what happened in the forest this afternoon.

KING DERAMO-TARTAGLIA: An explanation? Ah, the five hundred ducats! Well, after all, since none of you succeeded in bringing down the stag, I hardly think . . .

PANTALONE: Excuse me, sire. It's not the bounty that concerns us. If I may be permitted to remind Your Majesty, you killed a man today.

LEANDRO: Without provocation.

GENERAL SPAVENTO: Illegally, too, I might add.

KING DERAMO-TARTAGLIA: (*Getting an idea.*) Indeed? Perhaps you could describe this man—the one you say I killed?

PANTALONE: Surely you remember, sire! This afternoon, in the forest, an old hermit, stooped and frail . . .

GENERAL SPAVENTO: Gray hair, beard, a sorry looking chap, with . . .

KING DERAMO-TARTAGLIA: One moment, if you please. Before you go on . . . (*Moving to the prisoner's hiding place.*) . . . perhaps you can tell me: did this old hermit you accuse me of murdering . . . (*Yanking Old Hermit-King Deramo to his feet.*) . . . did he happen to look anything like . . . (*Pushes Old Hermit-King Deramo to center.*) . . . THIS? (*There is a shocked silence.*)

PANTALONE: Good heavens!

GENERAL SPAVENTO: It's the corpse!

LEANDRO: It can't be!

KING DERAMO-TARTAGLIA: I only wounded him. A slight flesh wound. And the only reason I shot him was . . . (*HE thinks hard.*)

PANTALONE: Was . . . ?

LEANDRO: Yes?

GENERAL SPAVENTO: I'm rather curious about that myself.

KING DERAMO-TARTAGLIA: Because . . . (*Inspired.*) . . . this is the man who killed my beloved Prime Minister, Tartaglia. I saw him do it!

CLARICE: My brother is dead?

KING DERAMO-TARTAGLIA: I regret to say, yes. A wonderful human being, a great statesman, gone. (*HE and CLARICE weep.*) Murdered by this wicked old man . . . (*Looks at Angela, thinks quickly.*) . . . and that vicious brute, Truffaldino. I was so overcome I c-couldn't k-keep a clear head. (*Pause.*) That's why I forgot to mention it till now.

GENERAL SPAVENTO: You see? I told you there was some perfectly logical explanation.

KING DERAMO-TARTAGLIA: And because this villain murdered my dearest, most trusted minister . . . (*Takes Leandro's sword.*) . . . I shall personally execute him.

(*Approaches the helpless Old Hermit-King Deramo.*) Say your prayers, old man. This is the end for you! (*HE starts to swing the sword. ANGELA steps between them.*)

ANGELA: No!

KING DERAMO-TARTAGLIA: Angela! Stand aside!

ANGELA: Doesn't he have the right to speak in his own defense?

PANTALONE: That's correct. He may be guilty, but he must be heard before he can be condemned. That's the law.

GENERAL SPAVENTO: Right-o. Fair play, all that.

LEANDRO: What harm can it do?

ANGELA: Please, sire. Let him speak.

KING DERAMO-TARTAGLIA: Very well. (*LEANDRO removes the Old Hermit's gag.*) But remember. He's a homicidal m-m-maniac! He'll say anything to save himself!

GENERAL SPAVENTO: Of course, sire. We'll let him talk, and we'll all listen. But we won't believe a word he says. Fair enough?

KING DERAMO-TARTAGLIA: Fair enough. (*Turns to Old Hermit-King Deramo.*) Well? What do you have to say for yourself? The floor is yours.

OLD HERMIT-KING DERAMO: I am . . . not what I seem to be.

GENERAL SPAVENTO: Right. You SEEM to be a harmless old man. You ARE a murderer. We all know that, old chap. Carry on.

OLD HERMIT-KING DERAMO: (*In desperation, HE points to King-Deramo-Tartaglia.*) He is not the King!

PANTALONE: Oh, dear, he IS in a bad way, isn't he?

GENERAL SPAVENTO: (*To the Old Hermit.*) Right. He is Charlemagne. And I'm Alexander the Great. I don't believe I caught YOUR name. Attila the Hun perhaps? (*To King Deramo-Tartaglia.*) You're right, sire. A lunatic. No question.

LEANDRO: Even so. (*To King Deramo-Tartaglia.*) If you say he killed Tartaglia, it's your word against his.

PANTALONE: The King's against a madman's.

SMERALDINA: Funny though. He doesn't look strong enough to kill a fly.

ANGELA: Let him talk. Go on, old man.

OLD HERMIT-KING DERAMO: (*Giving up.*) I can say nothing they would believe. Angela? (*SHE looks at him strangely.*) Before it's too late. I love you . . . as long as flowers bloom . . .

ANGELA: (*A dawning revelation.*) As long as flowers bloom and stars still shine?

OLD HERMIT-KING DERAMO: Yes. Farewell.

KING DERAMO-TARTAGLIA: Let's get to the execution!

ANGELA: (*To Old Hermit-King Deramo.*) Speak to them!

OLD HERMIT-KING DERAMO: What can I say?

ANGELA: Tell THEM what you told ME!

OLD HERMIT-KING DERAMO: What?

ANGELA: Something only you could know.

KING DERAMO-TARTAGLIA: Come on, come on, no more delays.

OLD HERMIT-KING DERAMO: (*HE moves quickly to each of the men in turn. KING DERAMO-TARTAGLIA watches him with increasing apprehension.*) My lord Pantalone, you were the old King's minister for fourteen years.

You've served his son for six. Neither one ever called you an "old fool." (*Points to KING DERAMO-TARTAGLIA.*) This man did today.

PANTALONE: So he did.

OLD HERMIT-KING DERAMO: General, Deramo once told you in private that he had chosen you as commander of the army not for your bravery, but for your cowardice. He said, "You hate to fight and so do I."

GENERAL SPAVENTO: Great Scott, his very words!

OLD HERMIT-KING DERAMO: Leandro, this morning Deramo suggested that if you wait until the Prime Minister's temper cools, you might yet marry Clarice. But look at him. (*Points to King Deramo-Tartaglia.*) His temper has not cooled, has it? (*Silence. ALL look at King Deramo-Tartaglia.*)

KING DERAMO-TARTAGLIA: What is it? You surely don't believe this nonsense!

ANGELA: Excuse me, sire. (*To the rest.*) It's time to cast your votes in this man's trial. Innocent or guilty. Each minister has a vote. According to protocol . . .

KING DERAMO-TARTAGLIA: According to protocol, the Prime Minister votes first. And the P-prime Minister votes . . . (*Thumb down.*) . . . guilty!

PANTALONE: What do you mean, sire?

ANGELA: Don't you see? (*Pointing to Old Hermit-King Deramo.*) He is Deramo!

GENERAL SPAVENTO: Impossible!

ANGELA: It's true!

PANTALONE: But why should you think that, child?

ANGELA: It's not his face. Or his voice. And yet, I know Deramo. His tenderness, his trust, his love. (*Points to King Deramo-Tartaglia.*) That man is not the King!

KING DERAMO-TARTAGLIA: She's crazy! This is all

a p-plot against me! You've always hated me, all of you! (*Refers to the General.*) This blustering old windbag! (*Refers to Pantalone.*) This jealous old man who w-wanted to be P-prime Minister! (*Refers to Leandro.*) This nobody who thought he could m-marry my sister! (*Realizes what he has said.*) I didn't mean that! I was only c-c-c-confused! Overc-c-c-come!

    GENERAL SPAVENTO: That stammer is familiar.

    PANTALONE: I certainly is.

    LEANDRO: Tartaglia! You're Tartaglia!

    KING DERAMO-TARTAGLIA: And you're d-d-dead! (*Lunges at Leandro with sword. LEANDRO, who is unarmed, evades HIM. A chase.*) I'll k-kill you all!

    PANTALONE: Do something, General!

    GENERAL SPAVENTO: Right. Retreat! Retreat!

    KING DERAMO-TARTAGLIA: (*Turning his attention to the General, at whom HE lunges.*) First you, windbag! (*A short duel ensues. ALL encourage the GENERAL, who fights reluctantly, chiefly by shouting at his opponent. Finally HE runs for cover, on the verge of a heart attack. ANGELA, meanwhile, has untied the Hermit's hands.*)

    LEANDRO: General, quick, your sword!

    KING DERAMO-TARTAGLIA: (*Lunging at him.*) Too late, b-boy! (*CLARICE tosses the General's sword to Leandro just before KING DERAMO-TARTAGLIA runs him through. LEANDRO quickly fences KING DERAMO-TARTAGLIA into submission and disarms him.*)

    PANTALONE: Enough, Leandro, enough. Everything seems to be under control now. Except . . . (*Moving to Angela and Old Hermit-King Deramo.*) . . . . how on earth did all this happen?

    OLD HERMIT-KING DERAMO: It was magic, my

friends.

GENERAL SPAVENTO: Magic! I knew we never should have invited that magician here! Didn't I say so?

KING DERAMO-TARTAGLIA: (*Being held at bay by LEANDRO.*) No, you didn't say so, you incompetent pea-brain!

LEANDRO: (*Threatening with his sword.*) Quiet!

OLD HERMIT-KING DERAMO: Using a magic spell given me by Norando, I entered the body of a king stag. Of course, it was my intention to return to my own body after a few hours. But Tartaglia knew the spell and took advantage of my trust to take over my body—the King's body— while I was cavorting around as the stag. (*ALL try hard to follow the story.*) So there I was, trapped in the body of a king stag. When Tartaglia killed the old hermit, whoever he was, poor soul, I decided to use the spell once again, and entered his body. And here I am.

GENERAL SPAVENTO: You see? That's the perfectly logical explanation I was talking about.

PANTALONE: But doesn't that mean that the only way you can return to your own body is by . . . killing him? (*HE looks at King Deramo-Tartaglia.*)

OLD HERMIT-KING DERAMO: It does.

LEANDRO: Then he shall die. (*LEANDRO moves as if to prepare for the kill.*)

CLARICE: No! Please!

OLD HERMIT-KING DERAMO: It's all right, Clarice. He won't be killed. There's been too much killing.

LEANDRO: But sire!

PANTALONE: Leandro, the King, in his wisdom, has made his choice.

GENERAL SPAVENTO: But what of his punishment,

sire?

OLD HERMIT-KING DERAMO: Exile. Like the old hermit, he shall live alone in the forest. (*Turns to Angela.*) And you, Angela, I release you from your vow. An old man is no fit husband for you.

ANGELA: (*In his arms.*) Deramo, my lord, my King . . .

KING DERAMO-TARTAGLIA: (*Rising.*) Aha! I have my revenge! Deramo is c-condemned to die an old m-man's death, while I . . . (*Indicating Deramo's body.*) . . . I have won! The last laugh is m-mine! (*He laughs wildly. The parrot's cry is heard. LIGHTNING, THUNDER, BLACKOUT. When LIGHTS come up, the parrot is missing and NORANDO THE GREAT has appeared in its place. EVERYONE ELSE is frozen in a tableau in the positions they held before the blackout.*)

NORANDO THE GREAT:

All creatures here are frozen still as ice.

I clap my hands once, twice and thrice . . .

(*BLACKOUT. When LIGHTS come up, tableau seems to be unchanged, except that OLD HERMIT-KING DERAMO and KING DERAMO-TARTAGLIA have been transformed into each other, feet to waist. In reality, doubles wearing life masks have taken the places of the "real" OLD HERMIT-KING DERAMO and the "real" KING DERAMO-TARTAGLIA, who have exited.*)

The evil deeds here wrought have been undone,

All darkness passed into the light of sun.

(*BLACKOUT. When LIGHTS come up, the transformation has extended to the characters' chests.*)

And when the harm my magic's done you lose,

My magic is no longer yours to use.

(*BLACKOUT. Statue crumbles. When LIGHTS come up,*

KING DERAMO is dressed as usual.   TARTAGLIA is still laughing, but HE is dressed in the Old Hermit's rags.   In reality, the doubles have exited and have been replaced by the "real" KING DERAMO and the "real" OLD HERMIT.)

PANTALONE: Sire! It's you again, isn't it?

KING DERAMO: (*Examining himself.*)   Deramo is himself again in every way. (*HE and ANGELA embrace.*)

NORANDO THE GREAT: Well, I'm glad to see that everything's back to normal. I must be going now.

OLD HERMIT-TARTAGLIA: (*Examining himself.*) No! (*To Norando the Great.*) What have you done, you miserable wretch! You've ruined everything! (*The OTHERS hoot, laugh and applaud.*) I'll get you yet, you stupid little toads!

KING DERAMO: You'll get what you deserve, Tartaglia: to live an old man's life, alone and broken. That's justice, isn't it, Norando?

NORANDO THE GREAT: That's for you to say, Your Majesty. My job is through.

KING DERAMO: A job well done.

NORANDO THE GREAT: I enjoyed every minute of it.

KING DERAMO: Every minute of it?

NORANDO THE GREAT: Yes, you may have noticed me about from time to time. On a tree in the forest . . . (*Pointing to the parrot perch.*) . . . right here in the garden.

OLD HERMIT-TARTAGLIA: The p-p-parrot!

NORANDO THE GREAT: An uncomfortable disguise. Next time I'll try something else. I must be on my way now.

KING DERAMO: But Norando, please . . .

NORANDO THE GREAT: You don't need me. You've found a far more powerful magician: Angela. After all, she saw what no mortal eye could see—the heart of Deramo.

KING DERAMO: But . . .

NORANDO THE GREAT: You must excuse me. I believe it's time for me to say: without hesitation, without preparation! (*THUNDER, LIGHTNING, BLACKOUT. When LIGHTS come up, Norando the Great has disappeared.*)

GENERAL SPAVENTO: Clever fellow, that.

KING DERAMO: But he was right. Not as clever as my Angela. (*Kisses her.*) Leandro, Clarice. Join us tomorrow. A double wedding!

LEANDRO: Clarice?

CLARICE: Oh, yes! Thank you, Your Majesty.

OLD HERMIT-TARTAGLIA: What are you talking about? Out of the question! I forbid it!

PANTALONE: You can't forbid anymore, Tartaglia. We know what you're really like.

GENERAL SPAVENTO: That's right, old chap. You're no good, you know. Rotten through and through.

CLARICE: He's still my brother.

PANTALONE: You're right, Clarice. Why don't we walk him to the edge of the forest?

GENERAL SPAVENTO: Capital! (*As OLD HERMIT-TARTAGLIA, CLARICE, LEANDRO, PANTALONE, and GENERAL SPAVENTO exit.*)

CLARICE: I'll bring you food every week.

LEANDRO: Perhaps you'd like to have some books.

GENERAL SPAVENTO: What do you fancy? A bird guide? Something on trees? (*THEY are gone.*)

KING DERAMO: Look, Angela. The stars are bright, the night is calm. Mother Nature seems to wish us well. (*THEY exit.*)

SMERALDINA: You know, I feel just a little bit depressed. (*A WHISTLE is heard from offstage.*)

TRUFFALDINO: (*Entering.*) Where is every . . . (*Spots

SMERALDINA, who has planted herself in his path.). . . body?
    SMERALDINA: Well, hello.
    TRUFFALDINO: Well, hello to you, too. You're just the person I was looking for.
    SMERALDINA: You don't say.
    TRUFFALDINO: Weren't we going to pick some flowers?
    SMERALDINA: We were.   Back when the sun was shining.
    TRUFFALDINO: There's the moon.
    SMERALDINA: Oh, yes, moonlight.
    TRUFFALDINO: We could give it a try.
    SMERALDINA: I suppose we could.
    TRUFFALDINO: Well, let's go. (*THEY turn to move upstage.   TRUFFALDINO sees that a note is attached to Smeraldina's back.*) Wait a minute.
    SMERALDINA: (*Stopping in her tracks.*) Don't tell me. Another message from what's-his-name?
    TRUFFALDINO: (*Removing the message from her back.*) How did you guess?
    SMERALDINA: Experience. Well, goodbye, Truffaldino. (*SHE starts out.*)
    TRUFFALDINO: No wait! It's the truth! Here, you can read it yourself. (*SHE strides back skeptically, pulls the note from his hand and reads.*)
    SMERALDINA: "Norando to Truffaldino."   (*To audience.*) I had an idea it would say that. (*Reads.*) "Am enjoying the sun on the island of Crete. Wish you were here. Join me as soon as possible."
    TRUFFALDINO: No, really?
    SMERALDINA: (*Handing him the note.*)   Really. (*Starting out.*) So long, pal.

TRUFFALDINO: Wait, there's more!   (*SHE stops.*) "You may bring Smeraldina with you if she wishes and if her father consents."

SMERALDINA: You're making that up.

TRUFFALDINO: Am not! It's right here! (*SHE returns.*) Do you?

SMERALDINA: What?

TRUFFALDINO: Wish.

SMERALDINA: I do.

TRUFFALDINO: Does he?

SMERALDINA: Does who?

TRUFFALDINO: Your father.

SMERALDINA: What?

TRUFFALDINO: Consent.

SMERALDINA: He's been trying to marry me off for years.

TRUFFALDINO: Good! How about we stick around for a couple of days and . . .

SMERALDINA: How about we stick around for one day? I know a double wedding we can turn into a triple!

TRUFFALDINO: Great! But wait. There's still a P.S. on this note.

SMERALDINA: (*Suspiciously.*) What does it say?

TRUFFALDINO: "P.S. - Please tell everyone goodbye for me." (*SMERALDINA and TRUFFALDINO wave goodbye to the audience. They are joined by the ENTIRE CAST.*)

ALL: Goodbye.   Come again.   Nice meeting you. Goodbye.

* * *

www.ingramcontent.com/pod-product-compliance
Lightning Source LLC
Chambersburg PA
CBHW070640120726
47909CB00004B/1513